IN BED W
A PERFECT STRANGER

A knocking on the stateroom door awoke
Paige from her deep and dreamless
sleep. Before she could say anything, the
door opened. A startled steward looked
into the room.

"I'm sorry, miss," he said. "I always bring
Mr. Winthrop's coffee now, and he didn't
tell me different."

He fled then, no doubt to spread the news
of what he had seen. Paige lying beside
John Winthrop in John's wide berth.

Paige didn't have time to tell him that it
had been an accident—and that John had
not touched her. She could only sigh. She
could only look at John still sleeping
peacefully, his long, lean form relaxed, his
handsome face smiling softly pressed
against the pillow. She could only wonder
what would happen now and in the days
and nights at sea to come. . . .

STOWAWAY
FOR
LOVE

Glenna Finley

A SIGNET BOOK

SIGNET
Published by the Penguin Group
Penguin Books USA Inc., 375 Hudson Street,
New York, New York 10014, U.S.A.
Penguin Books Ltd, 27 Wrights Lane,
London W8 5TZ, England
Penguin Books Australia Ltd, Ringwood,
Victoria, Australia
Penguin Books Canada Ltd, 10 Alcorn Avenue,
Toronto, Ontario, Canada M4V 3B2
Penguin Books (N.Z.) Ltd, 182–190 Wairau Road,
Auckland 10, New Zealand

Penguin Books Ltd, Registered Offices:
Harmondsworth, Middlesex, England

First published by Signet, an imprint of New American Library,
a division of Penguin Books USA Inc.

First Printing, March, 1992
10 9 8 7 6 5 4 3 2 1

PUBLISHER'S NOTE
This is a work of fiction. Names, characters, places, and incidents either
are the product of the author's imagination or are used fictitiously, and any
resemblance to actual persons, living or dead, events, or locales is entirely
coincidental.

For John

"Whoever loves, if he do not propose
  The right true end of love, he's one that goes
To sea for nothing but to make him sick."

—JOHN DONNE

Chapter One

SO MUCH FOR "restful sea cruises," Paige Collins thought resentfully, as she tried to wedge herself into a corner of the narrow padded bench along the wall of her stateroom and avoid hitting the floor.

It wasn't an altogether successful maneuver just then because the *MV Luella Eccles* was struggling through a Force 10 Atlantic storm that wasn't supposed to subside for another eight hours. The bow of the huge container ship was plunging into the towering waves with sickening regularity—finishing the process with an unladylike toss of her stern.

For the past two hours, Paige had been using positive thinking so that her stomach didn't follow the same pattern in her passenger cabin under the freighter's bridge on the port side. Ordinarily the location of the accommodation couldn't be faulted; it provided a marvelous view of the sea and came complete with her own deck space for sunbathing or solitude. That had been splendid for the six days since they'd left Norfolk, Paige thought, as the ship shuddered through another wave onslaught. Then the unexpected storm had arrived with winds that had already brought communication wires down outside her door, and would have sent the deck chairs flying if they hadn't already been lashed and stored away. Even the heavy metal cabin door that led from her stateroom out onto the deck rattled alarmingly under some of the heavier gusts.

For a moment Paige thought about the scarlet survival suit packed in a bag on the closet floor and the orange life jacket above it. That vision made her stomach give a warning rumble, and she hastily changed the direction of her thoughts. After all, the *Luella Eccles* had been fighting Atlantic storms for twenty-five years. Captain Griffin had proudly informed her of that on her first night aboard, and he certainly hadn't looked alarmed when she'd passed him in the corridor a few hours earlier.

The *Luella Eccles* rose again to cut through another wave, and Paige felt the ship shudder as the force of the Atlantic gale seemed to shove them sideways at the same time. The sound of the crockery hitting the floor nearby made her moan and chew on the edge of her lower lip so hard that she tasted a drop of blood. For an instant, she thought about going over to put her life jacket on, and then gave her head an angry shake. Just her luck to have the freighter's only other passenger appear on the scene if she did.

Not that she'd mind his materializing at that particular moment, she decided as the sound of the wind rose beyond the cabin door. If John Winthrop had even a drop of masculine gallantry in his body, he would have been knocking on her cabin door at the beginning of the storm to ask if she were all right. Although she couldn't imagine why she hoped for such consideration after a week of being left severely alone—ever since they'd left the Virginia coast and headed across the Atlantic for the English Channel.

Being ignored by men wasn't a state of affairs that often happened to Paige. At least, not since her late teens after her five-foot-four figure had fined down to whistle-bait measurements. When those were combined with a glossy mane of brown hair, a clear complexion, and a lovely smile, attracting men hadn't been a problem. Usually it was just the opposite. Certainly they didn't ignore her like the man in the next cabin. He'd merely taken one disparaging look at her when he came aboard the ship in Norfolk. A little later when he'd knocked on her stateroom door, it was to ask with visible impatience if the luggage stored in his suite belonged to her.

Paige had felt the guilty flush on her cheeks as she blurted out that she'd move it right away.

"I think I can manage that," John Winthrop had told her coolly, leaving his own bags in the narrow companionway to pointedly move her two suitcases out of his sitting room. "Where do you want them?" he asked as she still dithered by her door.

"Anywhere," she replied, flustered. His annoyed look made her forget her defense tactic that the steward had put her bags in the suite as a temporary measure after she'd unpacked, and they'd both forgotten to move them later.

She knew she was acting like an idiot, and lifted her chin as he pointedly waited for her to get out of the way so he could put the empty suitcases in her stateroom. She didn't stumble over the end of the nearest twin bed in trying for some vacant space, but she did manage to draw the chenille spread awry as she took refuge beside it. "I'm sorry you were inconvenienced," she said, as he put the bags down and turned to leave. "The captain told me there would be another passenger. I'm Paige Collins."

He nodded and hesitated for the barest moment, as if aware that he couldn't ignore that it was his turn for introductions. "John Winthrop," he acknowledged tersely, and started for the corridor again.

Any thought Paige might have had about further amenities died on her lips, as she watched his tall form disappear in the cabinway and, a moment later, heard the slam of his door.

"And the hell with you, chum!" Her angry exclamation was out before she knew it. So much for a happy trip and all that public-relations stuff about the free and easy companionship on freighters. She was almost tempted to go out and look at the door of her cabin again to see if someone had posted a "DANGER" or "QUARANTINED PREMISES" sign on it.

It hadn't helped that she'd acted like an overwhelmed idiot, she decided, even though the man would have rated a second glance from any woman with his lanky frame, dark hair, and the gray-eyed glance that had skewered her with its disinterest. His brown leather jacket looked soft and expensive, and the beige gabardine trousers had fitted without a wrinkle at his waist. Her quick estimate was that he was in his midthirties, although there was a weary cast to his features that made it difficult to be sure.

Probably because of a lurid past, she'd told herself, as she started to see the amusing possibilities. There was undoubtedly a woman in it, and she'd deserted him heartlessly so he'd taken to sea to forget his troubles. If he followed her script, he'd latch onto a bottle of bourbon and forget to show up for meals—a happening that occurred not infrequently among freighter passengers—or so she'd been told by veteran travelers. It came as a surprise then to find that John Winthrop seldom missed a meal, or so her steward reported when she mentioned casually that she hadn't seen her fellow passenger for breakfast or lunch the first day out.

"Oh, he's already eaten," Salvatore had reported cheerfully as he handed her a menu. "Helped himself to early breakfast, and then took coffee up to his cabin. He and the chief engineer will have lunch together. The chief has a microwave in his quarters and a little refrigerator. That way, he skips a lot of meals down here—prefers his own menu. He usually just shows when we have roast beef or steak scheduled."

Since the menu Paige was perusing showed fried catfish, a western omelet, and red beans with rice as the top choices, she could understand the chief's desertion. Also John Winthrop's. Obviously he'd learned the ropes on a previous voyage.

The remembrance of that menu didn't help the condition of Paige's stomach. It was already twisted in knots from fear of the storm, but even fleeting

thoughts of things like fried catfish added a
momentary touch of nausea.

Another gust of wind seemed to make the
freighter shudder more than usual. Paige got up
from the narrow wall divan where she'd been hud-
dling, and made her way carefully past the end of
the bed to go and stare out the side window. The
blasting north wind had eliminated any overcast,
so that the pale moonlight glimmered on the moun-
tainous waves. Paige gave a gasp of disbelief when
she saw white spindrift covering the ocean's surface as far as she could see, making the water look
like a field of snow with pulsating valleys and
ridges that shifted ominously.

"Oh, Lord," Paige muttered, feeling her stomach muscles tighten at the sight. For half a second,
she thought about the crew trying to lower a lifeboat into that maelstrom, and then turned deter-
mindedly away. The sooner she stopped trying to
think at all, the better off she'd be.

That left two alternatives: she could take a
motion pill and surrender to its soporific effect, or
leave the cabin and head toward the lounge, hoping the ship's motion wouldn't be so violent on the
lower deck.

The excursion to the lower deck won without a
real contest, since she suspected that any pill she
took at that moment wouldn't stay down long
enough to do any good.

She reached for a sweater that she'd tossed over
the end of the bed, and made her way to the cabin
door as the stateroom floor conveniently tilted that
way. Her reflection in the mirror on the door
showed that her gold slacks and cotton blouse

looked as if they'd been slept in—even if she hadn't closed an eye. For an instant, she hesitated, wondering if it was worth the trouble to attempt a quick repair job with a comb and lipstick. Then, as the ship's stern shuddered in its distinct corkscrew maneuver, she gulped and hastily went out into the companionway, hearing the metal stateroom door thud shut behind her as she made her way toward the stairwell.

To her left, the door to John Winthrop's suite was firmly closed, and Paige wrinkled her nose derisively as she gave it a quick glance in passing. Probably the man was sleeping comfortably in his bed, with life jackets under the mattress along one side so that he wouldn't fall out at the height of the storm.

At that moment, the freighter shuddered again under the onslaught of a wave on her beam, and there was the sound of crockery smashing from the passengers' tiny kitchen at the other side of the deck.

"Dear God!" Paige muttered, and clung to the railing at the top of the stairs leading down. Never again would she make disparaging remarks about bumpy airplane rides and the inconvenience of wearing a seat belt. She shot a quick look up the narrow stairway to her right, which led directly to the bridge, and wished for a moment that she dared go up and ask the officer on duty if the storm was as bad as she thought it was. Which would be one of the sillier questions of the decade, she told herself as she turned and made her way down the stairs toward the deck with the top officers' cabins.

That linoleum-covered corridor was deserted, too. The door leading to the chief mate's rooms was closed as was the door leading to the captain's. There was a note clipped to the latter and, after a quick glance to make sure she was unobserved, she read it quickly—hoping for a late weather report. Instead, it merely reported that one of the engineering crewmen had a toothache, and requested the captain to arrange for a dentist's appointment when they reached Bremerhaven.

Paige started down the hall again feeling sorry for the poor man who had to suffer through bad weather and a toothache to boot. Which showed that she should be grateful for small favors, she told herself. Her stomach might not feel great but, thank the Lord, there was nothing wrong with her molars!

The radio officer's door was shut tightly, but the sound of transmission could be heard even through the thick metal. Probably it would turn out that he was getting the scores from the NFL, so that the crew could find who won the weekly ship's pool. That conclusion made Paige feel more cheerful, but she still clutched both railings carefully as she made her way down two more decks toward the officers' lounge and dining area.

She pushed open the glass doors on the end where the lounge was located, and wasn't surprised to find it in complete darkness. Normally there would have been one or two of the younger officers sitting in front of the television watching a cowboy or mystery movie from the large collection of videotapes. She noticed that the bookcases were securely locked, to prevent the ship's library collection from spilling onto the floor when the freighter battled its way through the storm. Her glance lingered a little longer on the thick rope that secured the television set to its base. On her first night out, someone had volunteered the information that they'd had to tie it down, because their other set had gone hurtling across the lounge during a rough crossing.

Another mammoth wave made the stern of the freighter skitter like a nervous horse, and Paige hung onto the back of a bolted-down chair until the floor became almost level again. She shook her head wearily and carefully made her way around the corner into the good-size galley, with stainless-steel refrigerators lining one side and cupboards on the other. The dumbwaiter, which led down to the main galley a deck below, was locked, as were most of the doors around it. The coffeepot that was usually on a small stove to her right had been put in the stainless-steel sink on a damp towel, while the sugar and canned cream were securely stashed next to the empty burner.

Paige stood staring at it—wondering whether her stomach would be able to withstand the motion while she heated some water, or whether it would be safer to climb up those flights of stairs again and take to the couch in her stateroom.

The faint smell of coffee coming from a towel folded on the counter made her decide that it would be better to get out—and fast!

"What in the devil are you doing down here at this time of night?"

John Winthrop's impatient deep tones quickly

brought her head up. "What do you mean—what am I doing?"

Her annoyed reply came without a pause and only served to deepen the frown on his face. "You sound like a comedian who needs a straight man." Then, as he examined her pale face more intently, he went on in a milder voice. "I must say—you don't look like somebody in the middle of a comedy routine."

Of all the things he could have said, that remark wasn't what she wanted to hear. "Thanks very much," she said with as much dignity as possible under the circumstances. "Now, if you'll excuse me—"

He caught her elbow in an iron grip when she attempted to move past him. "Don't be a damned fool," he said tersely. "You most certainly couldn't make the first set of stairs—let alone four decks up. What did you come down here for?"

For about three seconds, Paige thought about telling him that it was absolutely none of his business, but a quick glance at his determined features made her discard that reply, saying instead, "I just wanted out of my cabin. I thought maybe a change of scene and a cup of tea might help." She shrugged then and added, "Frankly it isn't worth the bother."

"Think it'll stay down?" At her uncomprehending look he said impatiently, "The tea. Any nausea?"

A faint smile lightened her face momentarily. "It was so rough that I couldn't have made it to the bathroom. And I've been too scared to be sick in the bargain," she admitted. When the stern of the freighter rose and twisted in another corkscrew, she was thankful for the grip he kept on her elbow. "At least I was then. I thought this was going to be a restful sea voyage," she finished irritably.

His lips twitched at her bitter tone, but his voice was reassuring. "It's okay. You don't have to worry. We should be through the worst of this in another hour or so."

Her upward glance was more graphic than she knew. "Honest?"

His free palm went up in a mock salute. "Honest to God and hope to die."

"You didn't have to add that."

"Sorry. Slip of the tongue. Come on—you'd better go sit down, and I'll heat some water for a cup of tea." He was leading her out of the galley toward her place at the captain's table in the dining saloon as he spoke.

Normally there was a magnificent view of the ocean from the row of windows behind the table, but the sensible dining-room steward had closed all the drapes in the lounge, so that she didn't have to watch the turbulent waters.

Without thinking, she put her elbows on the table after John had deposited her in the chained-down chair. "Oh, damn! I forgot about the damp tablecloth," she said, sitting upright quickly and rubbing her wet elbows.

"You'll dry. Just sit there and think good thoughts or indulge in omphaloskepsis."

"Contemplating my navel would be dull at the best of times," she told him as he turned to go back to the galley.

"You're right. I wouldn't recommend dwelling on the state of your stomach right now."

He had disappeared around the corner of the galley before she could think of an answer. As she sat in the wooden chair, waiting for him to reappear, she decided that the storm hadn't had any visible effect on him. He looked formidable, but very much at ease in a crew-neck Irish sweater and brown cotton slacks. He certainly was more tanned and relaxed than when he'd boarded the ship in Norfolk. Sometime during the trip, he must have used a deck chair to catch some sun.

She raked back a lock of hair that had fallen over her cheek, and wished belatedly that she'd taken time to put on some lipstick before leaving her cabin.

The man had a habit of bestowing a quick head-to-toe glance that didn't miss a thing on the way. After noting her wrinkled outfit, he'd probably get around to recommending a good boutique when they arrived in Bremerhaven. If they ever did, Paige thought, drawing in a quick breath as the freighter mounted a tremendous wave, seemed to waver on top for a moment, and then plunged downward again. It wasn't the only thing crashing down. From the galley came the sound of metal hitting the floor, and some profanity that wasn't in any basic English course. Evidently John Winthrop was having trouble, too.

A sudden vision of him being burned on the electric element flashed through her mind. "Are you all right?" she called out in a high nervous voice.

His disgusted "Hell, yes" made her subside

again at the table. "This is just going to take a little longer," he added in explanation.

Paige thought about telling him not to bother, and then decided against it. Just then she wanted company, and while she might draw the line at Attila the Hun or Norman Bates—anyone else was welcome. And she certainly didn't have to worry about her fellow passenger making a pass at her just then, unless it was to hold her head over the nearest basin.

Basins were definitely not a good thing to dwell on, and Paige hastily shifted her train of thought to the man in the galley. Despite judicious and casual questioning of the steward and the chief mate about her fellow passenger's background, she knew very little more than the day he boarded. If the idea hadn't been absurd, she would have thought that the crew were deliberately cloaking his identity. Which just showed that the sea air was affecting her mind as well as her digestive system, she told herself.

At that moment, the mystery man came around the corner of the galley carefully carrying a steaming mug. "I hope you like your tea black," he said putting it down on the wet tablecloth in front of her.

She eyed the mug dubiously. "At this moment, I'm not sure that I even like tea."

He shot her a wary look. "Didn't you take a motion pill earlier?"

She shook her head. "When I finally thought about it, there was so much motion that I wasn't sure I could reach the bathroom without going on my hands and knees."

"Well, it's a little late for it now." He was hanging on to the built-in buffet on one side of the dining alcove as he pawed through a drawer and emerged with a cellophane-wrapped packet of soda crackers. Coming back to the table, he dropped them alongside the mug and then shot her a puzzled glance. "What's so funny?"

She held up the soggy paper napkin that had been wrapped around the cutlery at her place. "Sloshing water on the tablecloth keeps the china from sliding around, but it doesn't do much for paper napkins."

He managed a fleeting grin in response. "Use your sleeve. Amy Vanderbilt would understand."

Paige nodded and took a careful sip of the hot tea, keeping her by then damp elbows braced on the table so that she didn't spill it. "Aren't you having anything?" she asked, as he lingered under the archway that separated the captain's table from the larger room where the rest of the officers normally ate their meals.

John leaned against the divider, easily keeping his balance on the slanting floor. "No, thanks."

"You mean the motion's bothering you?" Without waiting for an answer, she went on hurriedly. "I'm sorry. You shouldn't have had to be in the galley to heat this water. Even the faintest smell of food isn't great. I noticed that earlier."

"Forget it. I had coffee up on the bridge a little while ago, and if I want to get any sleep for the rest of the night—I'd better let well enough alone."

Her eyes widened in surprise at his words. "You mean, you can actually contemplate sleeping during this—this—" At a loss for words, she gestured toward the drawn curtains that were hiding the maelstrom outside.

"I can't see much point in staying awake," he said matter-of-factly. "Can you?"

Her lips twitched in a semblance of a smile. "I guess I don't want to miss anything. Especially the 'Abandon Ship' alarm. The bosun told me the other day that the forward lifeboat on the starboard side had the best engine."

His eyes narrowed in amusement. "I'll have to remember that. However, in this weather, I wouldn't count on a successful launch for any lifeboat." At her involuntary groan, he added hastily, "Forget it. This ship can weather far worse storms than this, and the cargo's still snug and in place."

"You mean there's something I forgot to worry about?"

"Oh, yes. Every once in a while the Atlantic claims a container or two during a bad blow. That makes everybody very unhappy. You're supposed to arrive with the same number of containers that you started out with. Just like passengers."

"I'll remember and not commit suicide in that case," she said dryly. "I'd hate to upset the accounting department."

"Fine," he said in the same tone. "I'll pass the word along to the captain, and take that worry off his mind." He watched her manage a final swallow of tea after chewing on one of the crackers. "Now, you'd better let me take you back to your cabin, so you can get some rest for what's left of the night."

Feminine pride made Paige say, "I know you

mean well, but I really don't need a watchdog, and I don't want to listen to the wind howling outside my door up there."

"If you stay down here, you'll be tempted to peer through those curtains," he said, jerking his head toward the ones behind the table.

While the fabric was thick enough to be completely opaque, there was no disguising the noise of the waves as they battered the hull of the freighter. Another monster sent the stern high just then, until it slithered down again with the sideways motion that made Paige's stomach muscles clamp even tighter.

John must have been watching her reaction closer than she realized, because he pushed away from the archway and took hold of her elbow in one decisive motion, pulling her to her feet. With his free hand, he retrieved the almost empty mug from her fingers, and detoured into the galley just long enough to put it in the bottom of the deep stainless-steel sink atop a thick wet Turkish towel. "They may have to buy a few more pieces of china after tonight," he said calmly, keeping an iron grip on her as they left the lounge and headed for the metal stairway. "One thing about freighters," he added, as he directed her up the stairs ahead of him, "you get plenty of exercise. Not like cruise ships where everybody cheats and takes an elevator."

Paige decided she could keep the light conversation going as well as he could. "I know what you mean. I was stuck between decks in an elevator once just for a few minutes, and the whole thing seemed totally ridiculous considering it was in the middle of the Pacific Ocean." By then, they had reached the next deck and flight of stairs. She was going to pause for a minute, but John urged her gently but firmly upward.

"Hang on," he warned when the ship plowed deeply into a wave and made her teeter on the edge of a step. "This is no time to try for a broken hip."

She shuddered visibly. "Thanks very much for reminding me. I'd overlooked that possibility tonight."

"I'll bet it's the only one," he muttered.

"You mean—just because I'm not anxious to go back up to my luxury morgue."

He pulled her to a halt as they reached the top of the flight, which was outside the radio operator's office. From the silence beyond the closed door, Paige deduced that the man on duty wasn't hanging on every movement of the freighter as she was. As John's fingers stayed on her wrist, she glanced up to encounter his frowning gaze.

"You're really worried about this storm, aren't you?" he asked finally.

She shrugged. "If you must know, I'm terrified. I've been sitting in my stateroom for hours wondering if this damned ship is going to turn turtle every time one of those mammoth waves sloshes over the containers."

"But apparently you've been at sea before." Clearly he was trying to find a logical reason for her state of mind.

Paige shrugged again, and tried to make it easier for him. "It was good weather all the time then, and the only person who got seasick was a woman down in the laundry room. She turned green before we left the dock."

His lips twitched. "A case of mind over matter. You don't have to apologize for feeling queasy in this little blow."

"I decided I couldn't cope with getting in a lifeboat or a survival suit when I was seasick as well. I may, however, have to change my mind." The last came when she clutched the railing at her elbow as the freighter's bow went plunging downward again.

John waited until the deck was on a fairly even keel, before urging her along the deserted corridor, past the captain's cabin, to the last flight of stairs up to the passenger deck. "In that case, I think drastic measures are called for," he said, sending her up ahead of him.

"At this point, I'd consider practically anything except a cyanide pill," Paige said, as she neared the top of the stairs and heard sounds of the wind moaning under the bridge. She pulled up when they reached the narrow passenger-deck corridor. "Honestly, I think I'd rather go back down to the lounge."

"Nonsense," John said briskly, taking hold of her elbow again and maneuvering her through the doorway of his suite.

"What are you doing?" She stared around the darkened interior of his living area, and then blinked as he turned on the lamp at the desk.

"Sit down on that lounge," he said, emphasizing his order with a firm push toward the green leather davenport along the wall. "I want to make sure that the drapes are closed in the bedroom."

Paige watched with a weary glance as he made his way to the tiny hallway, past the bathroom to the bedroom beyond. She remembered the floor plan from earlier when the steward had parked her luggage in there. In addition to a more stable location in the center of the ship, the suite was considerably larger than the two separate, single cabins along either side. There was also a larger ticket price. She had debated only for a moment when she'd made her reservation, deciding she'd rather have the extra money for purchases abroad.

Now she wondered if she'd made the right decision. The sound of the wind was more muted, since the suite was insulated by the side cabins, and the center of the ship seemed more stable against the force of the waves hitting abeam. There wasn't any difference at all in the up-and-down motion, she decided, as she had to cling to the arm of the divan when the bow plowed deeply into the ocean.

John found her still clutching the furniture when he returned from the bedroom. He took one look and detoured back to the bathroom, emerging a couple minutes later with a glass of water in one hand and a small plastic bottle in the other. He sat down beside her on the divan and handed her the water, so he could shake out a small white pill from the bottle.

"What's that?" she asked apathetically.

His lips twitched. "Do you really care at this point?"

Paige felt the ship shudder again, and fought a desire to put her head down on the end of the sofa and close her eyes. "Naturally," she managed to say, and then met his mocking glance. "Not really," she amended.

"So I gathered." He dropped the pill into her

palm. "Actually this is for motion sickness, and you get a nice sound sleep in the bargain." When she opened her lips to protest, he went on decisively. "I give you my word that you won't miss any excitement—in the unlikely occurrence that anything exciting should happen. When I was up on the bridge awhile ago, the helmsman was complaining to the mate about the lunch menu for tomorrow. Then the steward arrived and reported that the captain was sound asleep in his cabin— that's why he brought the extra carafe of coffee up to the bridge. So your staying awake is like sitting on an airplane and watching to see if the wings will fall off."

"I've done that, too," she said wearily. "You make me feel like an utter fool."

"I don't mean to. If it's any consolation, I hear the bosun is seasick, and he's been going to sea for fifteen years."

"That's a very nice speech of reassurance," Paige said, putting the pill in her mouth and drinking some of the water to wash it down. "I suppose I'd better go back in my stateroom."

Evidently her comment didn't sound as convincing as she'd hoped, because he took the glass of water from her clasp and said, "Relax. I have room to spare in here, and my social schedule for the rest of the night is bare as a bone." He timed his departure back to the bathroom to get rid of the water glass between another giant wave, which saw the bow of the freighter dipping deeply again and caused the shuddering shake of the hull when the ship recovered. If he heard Paige's sudden indrawn breath, he didn't let on. When he came back, he settled in the leather chair in front of the walnut desk and swung around to face her, stretching out his long legs comfortably. "I've been wondering why you got on a ship like this in the first place."

Paige's first thought was that he'd had plenty of time earlier to satisfy his curiosity. It would have been easy; all he had to do was show up for a meal now and then instead of deliberately trying to avoid any encounter. She had enough pride to reply stiffly, "Don't tell me that the scuttlebutt has left any gaps in my biography."

He looked amused. "The only reports I heard were complimentary."

"And hardly of the kind to win over the Women's Movement." Having overheard a few discussions about the female sex when her deck chair had been in the shadow of the bridge a few days before, Paige knew that if she had been the subject of discussion, her IQ measurement wouldn't have been the one in question. At least she could stop worrying about that aspect with John at the moment. The avuncular glance he was bestowing was the same kind he'd give a mongrel puppy abandoned by the roadside in the rain.

Her train of thought was derailed by a mighty yawn, and she was slow in getting her hand up to cover it. "I'm sorry."

"No problem. You might as well lean back and be comfortable until that pill starts to work. Do you come from the East Coast?"

His sudden change of subject caught her unaware. "No. Why do you ask?"

He settled back in the chair, as if planning to

spend the night there. "No special reason. I was trying to remember what the captain said—something about your working in a museum."

"There are a few out West," she replied. She would like to have sounded more sarcastic, but her tongue didn't cooperate. "Actually," she managed to put in all the syllables, but it was an effort, "actually, we have one of the finest collections of Native American artifacts in the country."

The slight grin that appeared and then disappeared again showed that he wasn't particularly impressed. "You don't look like the kind of a woman who'd choose to spend her days in the basement of a museum cataloging arrowheads."

His casual comment was so close to the truth that Paige could feel the warmth spreading under her cheekbones. "They let me out occasionally. And besides, there aren't a lot of museum jobs available these days. I was an art history major in college. After graduation, it came as quite a blow that the Metropolitan Museum and National Gallery weren't panting to find a new curator."

His eyes narrowed as he surveyed her. "You don't look old enough to have been pounding the pavements long."

Her chin went up again. "I didn't pound the pavements at all. I had a friend in Seattle who told me about this job two years ago. Right after I graduated."

"And you've been there ever since?"

She wasn't sure that she liked the incredulity under his tone. "It has its interesting moments, and I've had a chance to pick up some graduate credits doing research."

"What kind of research?"

It suddenly occurred to Paige that she was the only one answering any questions, and the way she was feeling then, it was an effort to come up with any answers—let alone the right ones. Her fingers tightened on the arm of the divan as the ship wallowed, and she realized it was the first time she'd been aware of the storm since he'd given her the pill.

"I don't think this is a good time for me to play Twenty Questions," she told him, stifling an urge to yawn. "Besides, it's your turn to furnish some of the answers. The steward hasn't come through with a bit of information about you—no matter how many diplomatic leads I give him."

John leaned back still farther in his chair. "Exactly what would you like to know?"

She shook her head wearily. "I can't remember. Don't tell me anything now—I'll have forgotten it by tomorrow. If there *is* a tomorrow." The last came when the ship shuddered again. "Just promise me you'll wake me up if they ring the alarm to head for the lifeboats."

"If that happens, I promise to take you and your life jacket with me," he said solemnly.

"Good! Don't bother with my survival suit." Her words were getting slower and slower. "It was made for the Jolly Green Giant, I think. I keep meaning to tell the capt—"

John sat up quietly as her head suddenly lolled against the back of the divan. As the bow dug down again, he moved across to hold her limp body on the cushions, and then muttered a heartfelt "Damn!" as he realized it was only a stopgap measure. "Miss Collins," he said, and shook her shoulder. "Paige—can you hear me? You can't sleep here. There's no way to wedge you in."

A gentle breath touched his ear as he bent over her, but her eyelids didn't even flicker.

"Damn it to hell!" he muttered as he straightened beside her, keeping a firm arm around her waist as he thought about his predicament. Then, with a sigh, he got to his feet and pulled her limp body up beside him as he staggered toward his bedroom. If there hadn't been so much motion, he could have carried her, but there wasn't any use risking it. If they hit the floor, she'd wake up screaming and with good reason, he thought ruefully.

It was an effort to get her atop the bed, which was next to the wall. That solved the "roll out" problem as long as he sat on the other edge. If he'd only used his head, he could have wedged a couple of life jackets under the mattress before the pill had taken effect. As it was, it would be too much trouble, he decided, and reached across to the other bed for a pillow.

As he stretched out, he decided it was the first time that being longer than the six-foot bed frame came in handy. Not that he had planned to end up sharing his sleeping quarters aboard. Especially not with his fellow passenger. From the first day out, he had decided that the one thing he didn't need to collect on the ocean voyage was the attractive woman next door. Especially one who spent her life in the basement of a museum, for God's sake!

He yawned mightily as he thought about it, and

then decided he might as well get some sleep as long as he was acting as a temporary bodyguard. The inadvertent pun made him grin for a moment before his features sobered again. Next time, he'd let the chief steward handle Paige Collins's problems. After all, he was the officer in charge of the ship's passengers.

With that satisfying and smug conclusion, he braced himself the best he could against the footboard and fell asleep, convinced that the young woman beside him would see the wisdom of his decision when the storm finally died down.

Chapter Two

IT WAS AN insistent knocking that finally made Paige open her eyes hours later. She blinked in confusion as she struggled up on an elbow, wondering why it was such an effort.

As the cabin door opened, she was still staring around at the unfamiliar cabin and became slowly aware of the steward standing in the open doorway, looking equally confused.

"I'm sorry, miss," he got the words out with difficulty. "I always bring up Mr. Winthrop's coffee, and he didn't tell me different." He seemed to be having trouble keeping his eyes from her waist.

Paige, still groggy from the motion-sickness pill, finally glanced down where his gaze was centered, and gave a gasp of surprise to find a masculine arm holding her firmly anchored to the bed. She struggled upright with wide-open eyes then, and discovered that John evidently had decided to share the bed sometime during the night. He was still stretched out beside her sound asleep.

The sound of the breakfast tray being put on the lamp table beside the headboard brought her glance back up to the steward, who was hastily backing out of the stateroom. "If there's anything else you need—" he muttered even as he started to close the door again.

"I'll be sure to let you know," she finished the sentence grimly, as the door closed hastily behind the white-jacketed Salvatore. No wonder he was in a hurry, she thought as she sat wedged against the wall. News was thin in the middle of the ocean, and now Salvatore could regale people on every deck with this little item. And the more she protested, the more knowing smiles there'd be. "Oh, hell!" she muttered, and then tried to figure out how she could get out of bed without disturbing her recumbent host.

At least the weather seemed to have settled down, she thought, leaning over to pull the blind from the window above the bed and peer out into the sunlit morning. Her lips parted in amazement as she stared down into the water. There were still tremendous swells as the aftermath of the night's storm and the surface of the water looked as if someone had spilled a gigantic box of detergent as far as the eye could see. Apparently the spindrift from the waves hadn't dissipated even in the calmer seas, so the Atlantic, for a moment, bore a white frothy surface instead of the customary gray-green.

It was so unusual that Paige longed to discuss the phenomenon with somebody, and she looked down hopefully at the long masculine figure beside her. John Winthrop seemed deep in sleep, and his relaxed features made him look considerably younger than she'd thought. The dark brows had smoothed, and lines at the edge of that firm mouth were barely discernable.

She had no doubts that those lines of disapproval would reappear as soon as he surfaced and found that his unwanted bed partner was still on the scene.

It wasn't going to be easy to crawl over him, even though he was lying atop the covers, and she didn't have to worry about shifting him off a blanket. Apparently he'd made a token gesture of covering her, she discovered, as she moved her feet and found they were partially entangled in a small throw that passengers could use in deck chairs if the winds were on the nippy side.

She moved her feet out of it carefully, grimacing as she saw she was still wearing her shoes. At least, her unwilling host hadn't bothered with any of the amenities. She chewed on her lower lip at that revelation, trying to decide if she was annoyed at the lack of attention or grateful for it.

Then disgusted that she even thought of such things, she inched herself onto all fours and lifted one leg carefully over John's knees. She managed to clear him, and let out a sigh of relief as her searching foot found the floor of the cabin. Just one more maneuver and then she could escape to the solitude of her own stateroom.

Everything would have been fine if the freighter hadn't encountered a rogue wave, that lifted her bow from the accustomed rhythm and suddenly made the hull wallow like an overweight behemoth in the spindrift. It caught Paige in the middle of her delicate transfer, and instead of landing gracefully with the second foot on the floor, she capsized atop John's sleeping form.

He surfaced a lot faster than the freighter, letting out a startled yell, and would have thrown Paige onto the floor if she hadn't instinctively clutched his sweater.

"What in the devil—" he began irately when he finally focused on her face just a nose away.

"It's nothing—I'm sorry—I didn't mean to wake you up." Her words tumbled out almost as fast she slid off him and managed to stand upright beside the bed. "I thought I could get out without disturbing you," she continued desperately, watching him rake his fingers through his hair, as he swung his legs to the floor beside her and sat up on the edge of the mattress. "There was a big wave. Anyhow, I'm sorry."

"You don't have to keep saying that," he said, giving her an annoyed glance.

"Yes—well, I thought I'd better leave as soon as possible. Salvatore came in and caught us."

"What in the hell do you mean—caught us?"

"Oh, Lord." Her fingers brushed back her hair from her hot cheeks, as she suddenly became aware of her rumpled clothes.

"I asked you—"

"I know what you asked," she said, matching his irritation for the first time in sheer defense. "I just meant that Salvatore came in with coffee and found us practically in each other's arms. God knows what he's telling the rest of the crew by now."

A snort of disgust was John's reaction. "It doesn't take God to figure out that one." Then, yawning, he went on. "Oh, well—it's been pretty dull below decks this trip."

Her mouth fell open. "You mean, you don't even care?"

His eyebrows came together as he stared up at her. "What's the big deal? You were asleep. I was asleep. I presume you were still dressed. I know I was. Sounds like a G-rated movie to me. They don't toss you in the brig unless it's a lot worse than that."

"Very funny. Well, it may pump up your ego to be involved, but it doesn't do anything for mine. I don't even know how to start explaining."

"Why explain?" He yawned again and then got up to check out the thermos carafe of coffee.

"Well, for one thing, I was in a ridiculous position."

He shrugged. "You sound almost disappointed that nothing happened. Considering the weather and all, I thought sleep therapy was the only thing indicated. If I'd known you felt differently—"

"I didn't feel anything of the kind," Paige said, cutting him off abruptly. "That wasn't what I meant and you know it."

"So why all the fuss?" John made no attempt to hide his boredom with the subject. "Just let me know if you ever change your mind. In the meantime, your conscience is clear and mine certainly is." He shot her a considering look, as he mentioned that before shrugging and pouring coffee into the only cup. "Here," he said, handing it to her. "You look as if you could use something."

With that frank remark, it took considerable effort for Paige not to pour the steaming liquid over his arrogant head.

Quite possibly John recognized the train of her

thoughts, because he stepped back and gestured toward the bed again. "You'd better sit down and be comfortable. There's still some hangover from the storm by the feel of things."

Paige reluctantly did as he suggested. "That isn't the only hangover around." She sipped gingerly at the coffee.

"You probably forgot to eat yesterday after the blow started." He was pulling up the blinds to stare out at the sea on either side of the bow. "There's not much left of the storm now."

"That's one of the more civilized comments you've made this morning," Paige said. She took another sip of coffee and decided that it would stay down. As John turned back to face her again, she remembered her manners. "I'm sorry to have filched the only cup."

"That's okay. I was just going to say that I'll get another one from the passengers' galley," he said, starting for the door. "If there aren't any china ones left after last night, there are bound to be some paper ones on the shelf."

Paige took advantage of his absence to rearrange the pillows on the bed and make herself comfortable, while trying to decide what she'd say at breakfast if anyone came out and asked her how she'd weathered the storm.

John came back carrying a thick mug before she had decided on her alibi. "Stole this one from the bridge," he said calmly, as he poured himself some coffee and then sat down on the end of the bed facing her. "Apparently all of the containers made it through the night and are with us this morning."

"What makes me wonder if the captain might be

more concerned if a container went overboard than a passenger?"

"Have some more coffee," he chided, "and cheer up. The Eccles Line has an excellent safety record. They've even rescued people who were dumb enough to be on other ships."

"I know," she replied. "I've seen the plaques outside the lounge, and the chief told me about two rescues by the first night out. I was trying to remember them last night, but it really didn't help."

"And now you'll never know if that survival suit would have done the trick, after all."

"It may seem funny to you—" she said irritably before he cut in.

"A storm at sea is never funny. You're right about that. But you rise to the occasion so nicely."

"You couldn't resist the temptation," she finished for him.

"Something like that. Where are you off to now?" he asked when she stood up abruptly and went over to put her coffee cup on the tray. "Talking to you bears a decided resemblance to keeping company with a Mexican jumping bean."

"Unfortunately, I didn't jump out of your bed early enough this morning," she said with some bitterness, as she went toward the stateroom door.

"You sound disappointed."

"That's not funny," she said, whirling back to face him, and then put an unsteady hand up as her headache reacted to her sudden movement. "I'm sure your motives were great, but next time—just let me suffer, will you?"

It would have been a good exit line, if she hadn't opened the door into the corridor and found herself up against the tall, thin figure of the chief engineer.

He had his hand raised to knock, and it was with an apparent effort that he managed to avoid rapping his knuckles on her forehead. "So this is where you are."

His words were more of an accusation than a statement, and if Hans Deiber hadn't been so decent to her during the voyage, she would have replied with something more than a calm, "That's right. Were you looking for me?"

Hans was approaching forty with twenty years at sea behind him as well as a strict German upbringing, and he didn't appear to be impressed by her mild approach. Shoving his hands in the pockets of his khaki trousers, he surveyed her with an austere look on his thin face. "I heard that you weren't feeling well."

"Salvatore has been busy," John said, coming up behind her and leaning against the threshold. " 'Morning, Chief. After the storm last night, I thought you'd be sleeping in."

"Some of us have work to do."

The expressionless features of the man facing him apparently made the chief engineer try for a more diplomatic approach. "Sorry," he said brusquely, "it was a long night. That damned shaft bearing was acting up again."

John frowned at the announcement. "I thought you had that problem solved for the moment."

"So did I. We've contacted the factory in Germany, and they're supposed to meet us at the dock with replacement parts, but right now we're holding things together with rubber bands and chewing gum. If we have any more weather like last night, it could present difficulties."

"You're the first person who's mentioned there was a storm," Paige said. "I was beginning to think it was only a figment of my imagination."

"Or maybe you just had other things to occupy you," Hans said, giving her a look that didn't need interpreting.

Paige wanted to tell him that if she'd planned on a night of passion, she certainly would have waited for smooth seas and a partner who offered more than a cup of tea and a reluctant berth at the height of the storm.

"Right now, the only thing that's bothering me is trying to keep the top of my head from coming off," she told him. "I was on my way to find some aspirin, so if you'll excuse me—"

As she attempted to get past him in the doorway, he put out a detaining hand and then seemed to remember that John was still standing in the middle of the cabin. The chief managed a wintry smile in his direction before saying, "I'll probably see you at breakfast, but if you have any time later, I'd appreciate it if you could spare a few minutes with me down in my office."

He closed the cabin door without waiting for a reply and only then, released his clasp on Paige's arm.

Paige stared up at the middle-aged engineering officer in some bewilderment. "I wish somebody would tell me what's going on this morning. What in the dickens is the matter with you? You marched me out of there like a teenager who'd violated curfew."

A wave of red appeared on Hans's high cheek-bones, and he pulled himself erect. "Perhaps I was a little more severe than necessary—"

Paige turned and started down the narrow hall-way to her cabin door. "Make that a lot more severe."

"Paige, I'm sorry." He closed the distance be-tween them swiftly. "I just didn't think Lucius would approve."

Her expression didn't lighten at his explanation. "Considering that I just work for the professor and that he's currently in London, I don't really see what Lucius has to do with anything."

"That may be," Hans said, following her to her cabin doorway, "but I did promise that I'd look out for you aboard ship."

"You may be friends with my employer," Paige said, more annoyed than ever that she was being taken to task for something that hadn't even hap-pened, "but that doesn't give you the right to act as a heavy chaperon. I'm twenty-four years old, for Lord's sake."

"Even so—"

"Even so—nothing," she snapped, and then put up a hand to her aching head. "Look Hans," she said apologetically, "I know you meant well, but I was as safe with Mr. Winthrop last night as I would have been with my grandmother." She shook her head dispairingly and reached for the doorknob of her cabin. "Forget it. If I don't find aspirin pretty soon . . ." her voice trailed off as she opened the door.

He stepped back, looking apologetic for the first time. "I understand. I'm sorry, Paige. Will I see you at breakfast?"

She managed a thin smile over her shoulder. "Probably. I'll see how I feel after a shower and change of clothes."

"I'd definitely recommend some food." His authoritative tone was back again, but when Hans saw her stiffen, he added, "Take it from a veteran. We've all been seasick a time or two, and something in your stomach will help your cause along."

She managed to smile in response. "Okay. I'll take your word for it. Just don't get in my way if I leave the table in a hurry."

To her relief, a hot shower helped her state of mind and her headache. The motion of the freighter had calmed enough so that it was only necessary to prop herself gently in the corner of the shower stall to maintain her balance, and later she was able to get dressed in a vertical position rather than taking the safer route of sitting on the edge of her bed.

She was happy to see that Salvatore had straightened all the evidence of her occupation during the storm; the blanket had been removed from the couch, and pillows were put in their proper places. Even the cool green and white color scheme seemed more pleasing in the morning sunlight than it had been during the midnight hours. Paige took a final look at her beige slacks and checked blouse in the same shades, wondering if something brighter wouldn't have been a better choice. Despite a judicious use of blusher and lipstick, she still didn't come close to resembling a vital woman.

She turned from the mirror, letting out an exasperated sigh. She wasn't going to the captain's dinner aboard a cruise liner, for heaven's sake! Still feeling annoyed, she reached for the doorknob and went out into the companionway. The next second she had collided with a solid masculine form that took up most of the narrow hallway.

"Don't you know better than to dart around on a ship, for God's sake" came a familiar masculine voice.

Paige removed her nose from the front of John Winthrop's cable-knit sweater and stared balefully up at him. "What makes me think you'd tell me all about it even if I forgot?" she asked wearily. "Are you keeping watch on this deck now?"

"There's another thing you should remember—rude isn't funny," he told her, as he leaned against the wall and let his glance run over her. "If you really want to know, I came to make sure you had some breakfast."

Her eyebrows climbed in disbelief. "For the past week, you've done your damnedest to avoid even saying hello to me, and now suddenly you—" Her words broke off as she realized what she was saying. "I'm sorry," she managed finally. "You're not the only one who's acting out of character. I don't usually snarl at people who are trying to be nice to me."

He gave a reluctant chuckle. "Now you've spoiled the whole thing, and I'll have to continue in this new phase." He managed a travesty of a bow before offering his arm. "I'd be honored, Miss Collins, if I could escort you down to breakfast."

"I don't promise to be very good company."

"That's all right. If we don't speak to each other, it'll really confuse the gossips after Salvatore's report. It'll certainly confuse Hans," he added, motioning her ahead of him toward the stairway that led down to the next deck.

She pulled back at the head of the stairwell, which led directly down from the navigation bridge, to let the third mate precede them, but only after he'd nodded and given them both a quizzical look that showed the latest rumor had already made it around the ship.

Paige groaned slightly and leaned against the corridor wall, allowing the man plenty of time to get ahead of them so that she wouldn't have to make any more polite conversation.

"What in the devil was Hans so upset about earlier?" John asked when they finally went down the stairs. "Maybe I should warn you that he's just separated from his wife—not divorced."

"Oh, for Pete's sake!" Paige rounded on him irritably at the bottom. "This is beginning to sound like a soap opera. I don't give a hoot if he's separated from three wives all at the same time. The closest he's ever come, was helping me down the engine-room stairs in front of two other engineers."

John gave a wary look around them to make sure that the chief mate's door was closed and the captain's—a bit farther down the hallway. "Keep it down," he said in a muted tone, gesturing her toward the forward stairs. "Then tell me why he's coming up to check on you like a jealous boyfriend. I've never heard about him behaving that way before."

"And knowing the way gossip circulates on this

ship—I'm sure that the word would have gotten around if he had."

He ignored the bitterness in her tone and waited for her explanation.

"If you must know, he's an acquaintance of my boss. Between the two of them, they've evidently decided that I'm not old enough to be sent on a trip to Europe alone."

For the first time, John's severe expression softened. It was just for a moment, but Paige, who lingered at the top of the next steep stairway, nodded in resignation. "Ridiculous, isn't it?"

"Let's say unusual in this day and age," John said dryly. "I'm surprised he wasn't around last night to hold your hand."

"It probably never occurred to anybody that I was scared. And from the way Hans talked to me this morning, I don't believe he's convinced that's the reason I was in your cabin."

"In that case, it might help if we snarl at each other over the shredded wheat."

"Shredded wheat?" She paused halfway down the stairs, keeping a tight grip on the railing as she turned to look at him. "I'm not so sure that breakfast is a good idea, after all."

He gave her a gentle shove between the shoulders. "Relax. You'll be fine. Start with tea and toast. That's the usual drill. Besides," he added when she went slowly on down the last few stairs, "if you look pale and interesting—nobody will doubt your reasons for being in the wrong cabin this morning."

Despite his assurances, there was no ignoring the sudden lull in the conversation as they pushed open the heavy glass doors and stepped into the officers' lounge area. Two of the mates, the radioman and Pearl the dining-room stewardess, subjected them to a quick but thorough scrutiny before turning their attention to the food in front of them.

Paige swallowed and tried to ignore the smell of fried bacon, which was heavy in the small room, managing a thin smile as John nodded to the occupants and steered her purposefully toward the captain's dining area.

She was relieved to see that the long table was empty, and that the absence of place settings showed the captain and mate had either already eaten or were going to stay on the bridge. She sat down carefully in her chair, making sure that she didn't have to look out and see the huge green waves at the stern through the big windows.

Evidently the storm was being declared officially over because the damped-down tablecloths had been replaced by pristine dry ones.

"I'm glad to see that you made it down, honey." Pearl, the attractive black stewardess who was on her first trans-Atlantic job, followed her to the table. "I wasn't sure that I would. The chief steward had to sub for me in the crew's dining room at first breakfast. I think he was afraid that I'd put everybody off the idea of food if I showed up. How about a little tea and toast?"

"That'll be fine," Paige nodded, trying to sound as if that was just what she wanted.

"And you, Mr. Winthrop?" The stewardess's tone was arch.

It wasn't surprising, Paige thought as she carefully unfolded her napkin. He was the type of man who seemed to bring out that reaction from the opposite sex.

John hesitated and then, without looking at Paige, said, "Just juice, toast, and coffee."

"You don't have to give up eating because I'm still a little under the weather," Paige told him, putting out a hand to stop Pearl's exit to the galley.

"Nothing of the sort. I never eat a heavy breakfast."

"Why is it that you don't sound convincing?" Paige said wryly. "Do you want to try that again with a little more emphasis on the right words?"

"Okay—so be it. Bacon and eggs, Pearl. Maybe rye toast if there's any available. And if you eat in a hurry—" he told Paige as Pearl moved away toward the galley, "you won't have to act like the iron woman when mine arrives."

Paige gave him a reluctant grin. "Actually, I'm feeling better. Is it my imagination or is the motion subsiding?"

John ducked his head to peer out the side windows of the dining saloon and then sat back in his chair. "You're not imagining things. It looks as if we're about to enter the Channel, and while that can be rough at times—it should be an improvement on the storm we passed through. That one was headed down toward Portugal and the Med."

Paige held up her palms in a gesture of thanksgiving. "Hallelujah! I may recover enough to see Bremerhaven when we arrive, after all."

"In that case, I'd suggest a few more calories than you're planning on right now," John told her as Pearl came in with her cup of tea and a saucer piled with dry toast. "It won't hurt you to take it easy, though. Lunch is early enough to start expanding your menu." He watched her take a sip of tea before saying casually, "Are you going ashore alone in Bremerhaven, or is Hans playing the heavy chaperon there, too?"

Paige felt a flush of embarrassment on her pale cheeks, and tried to hide her unease by reaching for a jar of strawberry preserves that Pearl had just put in the center of the table. "Actually, he did mention something about taking me ashore, but that was before the problems in the engine room."

There was a resigned look on John's face as he leaned forward to study her. "We may be a little late putting into Bremerhaven. In fact, the way things were going the last time I was down below, I'm surprised that we aren't adrift off the Irish coast. However," he said rubbing the back of his head, "I may quarrel with Hans over his extracurricular duties, but he's one hell of an engineer."

The way John had hesitated over the words "extracurricular" didn't leave any doubt in Paige's mind as to the way his thoughts were running. She broke off another piece of toast and managed to take a small bite even though her appetite had deserted her once again. "If we're late getting into Bremerhaven, I suppose that means we'll miss our scheduled arrival time in England afterward."

"That's right." For all of John's relaxed stance, he was watching her closely. "Will that cause you any trouble?"

"Not trouble exactly. After all, freighter schedules are late all the time," Paige responded, trying to sound as if it didn't matter.

"Not really. This is a blue ribbon run. Most of the time the line's customers can set their watches by our"—he paused then and hastily changed his words—"by the Eccles Line schedule."

Paige's eyebrows climbed. "You started to say 'our line,' " she said, meeting his glance squarely. "Does that mean you're a member of the staff here?"

He shook his head. "It's the first time I've even been aboard the *Luella*. One of the lines I worked for a few years ago shared cargo with the Eccles fleet on some of the runs. That's how I got to know Hans and some of the others."

"I see." She would have liked to ask him exactly what he was doing at the moment, but one night's acquaintance, no matter how informal, didn't give her the right to any deliberate probing.

Fortunately, Pearl came bustling back into the room at that moment carrying his plate of bacon and eggs in one hand and a saucer piled with toast in her other. "I'll bring some more coffee right away," she promised, and then glanced across the table at Paige. "How about you? Going to change your mind and have a few more calories?"

"No thanks." Paige was glad to find that her stomach had settled down to its more normal state, and the sight and smell of bacon didn't cause any trouble. Even so, there was no point taking chances. "I'll make up for it at lunch," she promised Pearl, who gave a satisfied nod before going to the galley.

She was back a couple of minutes later with a

carafe of coffee, which she put at John's elbow. "I'll let you serve yourself if that's all right," she told him. "I told the chief steward I'd check out some stores with him since he had to do double duty for me earlier."

"Sure, go ahead," John told her. "If we need anything more, we'll find it in the galley."

"Thanks." She gave them both a grateful smile and disappeared again.

"That's one of the nice things about a freighter," Paige said. "It's great to be able to raid the refrigerator at all hours. I've probably gained five pounds since I came aboard." She made a wry grimace. "Until last night."

"Don't dwell on that," John said in a firm voice. "Have another piece of toast. Then, after you're finished—you'd better go up and see if you can catch up on your sleep."

"I thought I'd already taken care of that," Paige said, glancing up from putting jelly on a bite of toast to give him a puzzled look. "About eight hours ago, if I remember right."

"You didn't rest very well." He kept his attention determinedly on his food, as he went on to say, "That's why I wedged you in. You would have been on the floor in the first fifteen minutes if I hadn't."

Paige felt an embarrassed flush go up her cheeks, and thought it was a pity that Hans hadn't been around to hear that declaration so her name could be cleared. Maybe if she asked, John would put up a proclamation to that effect on the lounge bulletin board, and she could go ashore with a dull, but unblemished reputation.

"Now what's the matter?"

His irritable question penetrated her woolgathering. "What do you mean?"

"I just wanted to know why you were giving that slice of toast such a dirty look. Look—if you're not feeling well—" he was getting hastily to his feet as he spoke, "—we'd better get you back to—"

"I'm perfectly fine," she snapped, cutting ruthlessly into his warning. "Sit down and finish your breakfast."

John subsided slowly into his chair again; the expression on his face carefully noncommittal. It was clear that he wasn't used to following feminine dictates of any kind—certainly not the manner in which she'd just spoken. His eyes narrowed as he surveyed her rebellious face. "What in the devil's gotten into you?"

His words came out like slivers of ice, but Paige didn't look back down.

"Not a thing," she said, dusting toast crumbs from her fingers and taking a final sip of tea before she stood up.

John shoved back his own chair and got to his feet slowly.

She managed a thin smile. "If you'll excuse me—"

"Do I have a choice?"

His annoyed question caught her before she'd taken more than a step, and she looked uncertainly back over her shoulder. Something in her expression must have touched a vulnerable chord, because the anger faded from his face. "Never mind. I'll talk to you later."

From his tone, Paige concluded that the conversation would only be held during bankers' hours and in the safe company of half the crew of the *Luella Eccles*. She managed to say, "I'll look forward to it," knowing that it sounded as if she'd have trouble fitting him into her busy schedule.

As an exit line, it wasn't too bad. And it should have given her feminine ego a much needed boost.

It was hard to understand why she felt so miserable when she crawled into her bed five minutes later. It was even more disturbing to find tears running down her cheeks, before her eyes closed and sleep finally gave her a blessed respite.

Chapter Three

CONSIDERING ALL THAT had happened on the voyage, the ship's arrival a day and a half later in Bremerhaven was almost anticlimactic. Paige awoke to find a surprising silence aboard the ship, which meant they must be docked at the German port with prospects for a day ashore. She turned over in bed and stretched luxuriously, thinking of all that had occurred after the storm, or rather hadn't occurred.

John's behavior had been impeccable, if that meant that he used every strategy to avoid being alone with her. There had been one fairly close call when he had come down the outside stairway from the navigation bridge, and discovered her reading in a deck chair just outside her stateroom.

That prompted a torrid exchange of greetings, which included the sunny weather, how the Channel now resembled a backyard pond, as if to make up for earlier transgressions, and that the *Luella Eccles* had made up some lost time, so Paige needn't worry about too much delay on the sailing schedule.

Paige noted a deliberate avoidance of her state of health, her current relationship with Hans, or what she planned to do on her free day in Bremerhaven.

Paige sat through dinner that night with only the captain at her side. He was a nice gray-haired gentleman who was probably wishing he was at the all-male, "invitation only," engineers' barbecue on the deck below. Unfortunately he had to make sure the only paying customer aboard was kept happy. They'd gotten through dinner with side tidbits of his thirty years at sea before he'd corralled Paige into watching a cowboy movie in the lounge after dessert. It seemed a lifetime before the hero and the horse melted into the sunset and Paige could excuse herself, saying that she wanted a good night's sleep so that she'd be all set to go ashore in the German port city.

Considering how long she'd been anticipating her first look at Bremerhaven, it didn't make much sense for her to be lying abed behind drawn curtains at her cabin windows. She sat up then and swung her legs over the side of the mattress. As she shrugged into her robe, she was thinking that the air-conditioning system was playing up again. The temperature in her stateroom seemed to fluctuate between near-freezing and suffocation with very little in between. Hans had sent a whole crew of his engineers to try and adjust the ceiling duct on the voyage, but the adjustments were short-lived. The way things felt at the moment, they might have been docked somewhere in West Africa instead of a German city where the temperature was now in the sixties.

"My Lord, it's hot," Paige muttered to herself, pulling her travel robe off again and tossing it to the foot of her bed. It couldn't be that bad outside, she reasoned, as she adjusted the venetian blind so that she could peer onto the bow. The scene below made her draw a sharp breath of amazement. There were longshoremen clambering over the big containers like ants—only six-foot ones wearing down vests and hard hats, as they gestured to the two crane operators overhead who were picking up the containers and lowering them onto waiting trucks on the pier without a wasted motion. She stood on tiptoe to see beyond the cranes, and noted the neatly stacked containers that would be put aboard the ship later on in the day. Her gaze shifted back to the men working the cargo, and she shook her head in amazement as they seemed to move nonchalantly from one container to another—loosening steel rods and preparing the big boxes for the unloading onto the docks. She let out a sigh of relief when she noticed the safety lines each man was wearing—much like high-wire artists in a circus. And when she saw the potential danger lurking with a misstep, it was understandable.

At that moment, one crew had evidently finished unloading a certain area, and the crane operator hoisted an openwork steel crate and put it down neatly beside them. The four men stepped inside and fastened the door. A moment later they were hoisted up and then put down on the dock. This time, she noted, they weren't put down on a flat-bed truck but in a loading area off to the side. The men calmly stepped out and headed down the dock, disappearing between two stacks of containers.

The man in the crane was already back to work,

handling two other longshoremen who were busy in another hold at the bow.

A sudden knocking on her door made her turn in surprise, and then go over to open it just far enough to peer around the edge. Pearl was standing in the corridor with an insulated carafe.

"Morning," she said cheerfully. "I brought some coffee to Mr. Winthrop, and I thought maybe you could use some, too." Her smile broadened. "If you're like I am—all those shops ashore are beckoning, and I don't want to waste any time aboard."

"That must be what's been bothering me this week," Paige said with a smile. "Shopping mall withdrawal symptoms. I was a fool not to recognize them."

"Then you take the coffee, and I'll bring you a cup and saucer from the passengers' kitchen. Won't be a second."

Paige did as she asked, leaving the stateroom door carefully fastened open so the stewardess could get in easily. She was back in a jiffy, carrying an extra saucer with a cinnamon roll on it. "I'd forgotten that we had these from the bridge watch last night," she said, putting it down alongside the coffee. "Don't let it spoil your breakfast though."

Paige shook her head after noting the size of the roll. "Don't be silly. This *is* my breakfast. I won't need anything more until a late lunch." As she followed Pearl to the door, she asked casually, "Are most of the crew going ashore?"

Pearl nodded. "Those that aren't on watch. The ones that miss Bremerhaven will get leave while we're in England. A few lucky ones will make both ports." She unhooked the door and then lingered on the threshold. "I wouldn't count on the engineers, though. They've got major repairs, I guess. A factory representative was waiting on the dock with replacement parts. He flew from Hamburg last night, they said."

"How do they arrange those things?"

"By phone," Pearl said matter-of-factly. "Everything's easy these days. The captain's been phoning his wife every night. He's trying to get her to come along on the next trip."

Paige's eyebrows climbed in surprise. "Good enough, I hope it works out for them. Thanks again for the breakfast. Maybe I'll see you in town."

"Right." Pearl gave her a jaunty wave and disappeared down the stateroom corridor.

Before Paige was able to close her cabin door, John emerged from the suite down the hallway to her left. He pulled up short at seeing her pajama-clad figure. "What's going on now?" he drawled in a resigned tone.

"Very little," Paige snapped, aware that her rumpled pale green cotton pajamas didn't make much of a fashion statement either. She deliberately stepped behind the door and said briefly, "Pearl just brought up some coffee."

"I take it that you're going ashore."

It was a statement, not a question, and caught her as she was closing the door. She pulled it open again just far enough to peer around it. "I planned on it. Why?"

"Are you going alone or is Hans riding shotgun?"

"From what I hear, he's going steady with a

piece of machinery in the engine room. I'll try to muddle along on my own." She managed to keep a light, uncaring tone. "Are you going into town later on?"

He frowned suddenly. "I'm not sure. It depends on some things."

"Well—" Paige caught herself before she uttered the cliché of "have a nice day" and managed to say instead, "Excuse me, I'm running a little behind schedule," before she closed the door.

Once it was safely latched, she leaned her forehead against the cool metal, and found that she was breathing as fast as if she'd just taken the stairs from the lower decks two at a time. She shook her head irritably, and then turned to survey her reflection in the mirror over the combination dressing table/desk. Her cotton pajamas looked just as rumpled as she'd feared. And her hair was in exactly the same condition, she discovered. "Damnation," she muttered as she went over to pour the coffee and take a sip. Why hadn't she stayed in her cabin instead of lolling against the door frame to wave good-bye to Pearl? Or why hadn't John done the decent thing and just waved casually before disappearing down the stairs? He was obviously all ready for a day ashore in suntan slacks and a dark brown turtleneck shirt under a V-neck sweater.

"The hell with it!" Paige muttered, taking another swallow of coffee before heading for the shower.

Twenty minutes later, her appearance was more presentable. She'd chosen a royal blue dress with a shirtwaist bodice, but a pleated skirt that was flattering and comfortable for walking. Her matching cashmere cardigan could be tied at her waist if the sun stayed out, or shrugged on if it didn't. The weather forecast was for a glorious early fall day, and a quick peek out at the dock confirmed it.

She slipped her sunglasses into her burgundy shoulder bag, which matched her low-heeled pumps, and took a quick look around the cabin. She had her traveler's checks and passport—and obviously the ship had been cleared by authorities so there was nothing to keep her from going ashore.

Paige had successfully negotiated the stairs down three decks, and was just making her way to the top of the gangway when she heard Hans's deep voice behind her.

"You're not going ashore so soon, are you?"

Pulling to a stop to let him catch up with her, she deliberately ignored his annoyed tone and said with a smile, "I thought I was being patient. Most women would have been in town by the time the shops opened." As she noted his wrinkled khaki uniform and tired features, her voice softened. "You don't look as if you got much sleep last night."

His thin lips settled in an ominous line. "I didn't even see the inside of my cabin after midnight. You're lucky that you woke up in Bremerhaven. For a while, I thought I'd be suggesting you get off and row."

"That bad?"

He struck his balled fist into his palm. "The whole damned ship should be scrapped if they won't allow me to replace the worn machinery.

I've told them over and over again. This time, we're lucky we could get the needed spare parts, except that we'll have to work all day installing them."

"That means you won't have any time ashore?" Paige tried to sound regretful without giving him the idea that her day would be ruined if she had to explore Bremerhaven on her own. As pleasant as his company had been on board, his sudden role change to a heavy chaperon wasn't welcome.

"Well, certainly not this morning." He gave her a sharp glance. "Are you just going to be wandering around on your own?"

"That's right." She waved a brochure of the town she'd found in the lounge the night before. "The place isn't big enough for much exploring. Besides, I would like to go shopping for clothes." Paige added the last as a deterrent, knowing that most men would prefer a dentist's appointment to a day wandering around dress departments.

Apparently Hans wasn't any exception. His suspicious look vanished immediately, and he said, "Well, I don't see how you can get in any trouble doing that. Have a good time. Maybe you'll be back early so that we can go out somewhere to dinner."

"Let's leave it open," Paige said hastily. "After all, you might still be working down below."

"I certainly will be if I don't get started," he said. "Don't spend all your money."

She smiled dutifully at his cliché—heavy as it was—and then gave a sigh of relief as he disappeared through the door en route to the ship's innards. Paige felt a moment's pang of conscience as she started down the gangway, knowing very well that clothes were the last thing she planned to survey in Bremerhaven. Even if London's stores weren't just a few days away, she wouldn't be tempted by German apparel.

There was a piercing wolf whistle that almost made her stumble on the last step of the gangway, and she glanced over her shoulder to see two of the freighter's crew giving her a friendly wave. She waved back, aware that even in that short time, she'd become part of the ship's family.

It was a wonderful feeling to put her feet on dry land, although the first few steps showed that the ground had a slight tendency to come up and meet her just like the deck of the ship. She didn't have time to consider the feeling, instead trying to make sure that she wasn't run down by the fork-lifts and truck traffic on the busy pier. Since the *Luella Eccles* was just one of a line of freighters tied up that morning, the regimented bustle was almost unbelievable.

She made her way toward a nearby stack of containers where the bosun had told her to wait for the port's shuttle bus to the gate. There was a tall, fair-haired man waiting as well, and he gave her a pleasant smile as she came up beside him.

"I saw you getting off the *Luella*," he said with an accent that was British rather than German. "Are you passenger or crew?"

"Passenger," she assured him. "Do you have any idea how long until the shuttle bus comes?"

"I'm not sure," he told her with an approving glance. "But it shouldn't be long. I just came down to visit a friend of mine on that ship tied up behind yours, but I didn't make connections. Apparently he's decided to take leave for this trip."

Since he was a nice-looking man in his late thirties, Paige decided to continue the conversation. "That must mean that you live in this part of the world—or are you just visiting, too?"

"I've been living here for the better part of three years," he said, and then broke off as a small bus rumbled down the pier. At his signal, it pulled to a stop beside them.

As he waved Paige up the steps ahead of him, she peered back anxiously over her shoulder. "Help—I forgot to get any German marks. Is there a charge?"

The driver apparently overheard and cut in briskly. *"Nein, fraulein.* No charge to the front gate."

"Here—sit down in this front seat," her new-found acquaintance waved her to the side after nodding to the only other passenger who was sitting toward the rear.

The bus started up with a jerk after they were both seated, and her seatmate continued, "As I was saying—Bremerhaven almost seems like home now. It's not very large, but there are some interesting things for visitors. I take it this is your first visit?"

"That's right," Paige said. "And I'll have to move fast because we sail before midnight." Even as she replied, her gaze was on the busy pier beyond the bus windows. There wasn't a vacant spot between the freighters tied up to the left, and in one case where tugs were nudging a Dutch ship out into the Channel, another freighter was being pushed upstream nearby to take the recently vacated space. "I had no idea this was such a busy port," she murmured. "It makes Norfolk or New Orleans look like the minor leagues."

"Minor leagues?"

Apparently his excellent English didn't include baseball, Paige thought as she turned back to explain, "Small towns. I've heard about European efficiency—this port is proof positive."

"Ah, yes." He beamed approvingly. "I would like to show you more of our industrial development if you have the time."

Paige frowned slightly. He was nicely dressed and apparently knew all the right things to say in his almost British accent, but she wasn't in the habit of being picked up on a pier or anywhere else.

Just then the bus slowed to a stop in front of the big front gate of the pier. The driver gave them an amiable nod as they descended, and had driven off again before they had taken more than a step or two on the cement walk alongside the port office building.

Paige saw a parking lot full of small European and Japanese cars, but she didn't see the taxi rank she had expected. At that moment, a taxi drove up with a squeal of brakes to the corner of the building, and she saw her chance of an easy escape. "I'm sorry," she began with a smile up at the man sticking close beside her, "but I'd really made other plans—" The sight of a familiar figure opening the taxi door made her words gurgle to a stop. Apparently John Winthrop had already arranged for possession of the only taxi around.

He was just about to get in when he caught sight of Paige and her newfound escort. His eyes widened in surprise for just an instant, and then his features took on the noncommittal expression that seemed to be a permanent feature whenever Paige drew near. "Well, well," he said keeping the cab door open. "Bo-Peep, as I live and breathe. It looks as if you've changed your mind for your day ashore."

Paige gave him a puzzled look, trying to figure out the Bo-Peep accusation. Surely he didn't think the man beside her was a sheep she'd collected on the way. And why was he being so unpleasant? It wasn't as if he'd offered to take her sightseeing. Just the opposite. Suddenly feminine pride took over. "Mr. Winthrop as I live and breathe," she said with a smile that was as synthetic as her tone of goodwill. "It looks as if the whole passenger list has deserted the ship, doesn't it? It's too bad that you've already hired a cab—otherwise perhaps you could have joined forces with us." She turned then to glance up at the man beside her. "Where did you say you'd parked your car?"

His English was good enough that he didn't hesitate a minute, taking her elbow and saying smoothly, "It's that gray one over there at the end of the row."

"Right. We'll be going then." Paige lingered just long enough to say sweetly to John, "I do hope you have a nice day. See you later." As she turned her back and walked down to the parked car her new acquaintance had pointed out, she heard the slam of the taxi door and a squeal of tires as John had evidently told the driver the German equivalent of "move it!"

By then, the man from the dock had the door of his car open. Paige's common sense returned before she stepped inside. "I'd appreciate a ride into the city," she said, "but I'd really just planned a day of shopping instead of sightseeing."

"I understand." He smiled down at her. "Even if your friend didn't. Incidentally, I'm Heinrich Schmidt."

Paige shook his extended hand. "Paige Collins. Thank you very much for helping me out. I took quite a chance."

"How is that?"

"It suddenly occurred to me that maybe you'd come by taxi, too. I would have looked like an awful fool it we'd had to beg a ride in his cab."

Heinrich gave a snort of laughter and closed the door after her, going around to slide behind the wheel before asking, "Is this a special feud you have with the man?"

"Not really," she said uncomfortably. "Why do you ask?"

"I did not understand his comment about Bo-Peep."

Paige said lightly, "Just a nickname," and was relieved that he merely nodded before starting the car and pulling out toward the two-lane highway in front of the dock area.

It was a beautiful fall morning, Paige thought, as he merged with the traffic and accelerated. There were some shade trees alongside the road, even though it was obviously an industrial area. The traffic consisted mainly of car carrier trucks, and it was easy to see why a moment later, as they slowed to allow one to turn into a tremendous dock area filled with small Japanese cars. "I thought they mostly went to the United States," she said, gesturing toward the busy terminal where the automobiles were being loaded.

"*Nein.*" Heinrich pursed his lips thoughtfully as he glanced at the loading area before stepping on the accelerator again once the car carrier was out of the way. "These imports are a big part of our economy. Not very popular with the people who like German products, but what can you do? Now, over there to the left," he said, gesturing with one hand, "is the old part of town. If you had more time," he glanced across to see her shake her head, "never mind, I'll take you to the center of the city. At least, I can persuade you to have a coffee before you start looking at the shops."

Paige gave a soft sigh of relief as he turned at an intersection and followed the traffic to what was obviously the main road to the city center. Despite her uneasiness about getting in a car with a stranger, the man was going to do as she'd asked. Sharing a cup of coffee with him was the least she could do to keep up her end of the bargain.

By then, the small, scattered buildings alongside the roadway had turned into a solid line of neighborhood shops, and just a few minutes later they were obviously in the center of town.

Heinrich found a parking space near a three-story building, which looked to be one of the better hotels if the discreet notices of the Michelin guide alongside the door were to be believed. He led the way to a group of white metal tables alongside the building where several couples were already enjoying morning coffee in the sunshine.

"Is this to your liking?" he asked as he started to pull out a chair for her.

Her lips twitched at his formal phrasing, but she didn't let on as she nodded and sat down, saying happily, "This is a wonderful idea. Early morning coffee aboard the ship was quite awhile ago, and I'll need something to get me through all the walking I've planned."

"Good—good." As a white-jacketed waiter approached, Heinrich said solicitously, "And how about something to go with it? A roll? Croissant? They have a French pastry chef here so it is good."

"I'm sure it is," she replied but shook her head. "Just coffee please." And then remembering how strong the Europeans liked it, "With cream."

Paige lingered with him over two cups of coffee, hearing him tell about the places she should visit during the day before finally glancing at her watch. "I should be moving along," she said pushing back her chair and getting to her feet. "You've been very kind, Heinrich."

"I wish I could persuade you to have dinner and spend the evening with me," he said, reluctantly standing up.

"I'd better not. You know how they are about changing the sailing schedule," she said, improvising to find a good excuse. "The captain's very strict about passengers being on board in plenty of time."

"If you insist." He bent over her obviously intent on a farewell kiss. Paige reacted automatically, stepping back and putting her hand against his chest.

He grimaced, then caught her fingers, and brought them to his lips. "Not good-bye, my dear—just *auf Wiedersehen.*"

She retrieved her fingers with a slight struggle, managed another smile, and turned toward the main pedestrian mall alongside the hotel. Once he was out of sight, she gave a sigh of relief. Thank heavens, he hadn't persisted in his theatrical farewell. Obviously he'd seen too many American movies and had stored away the dialogue for future use.

She slowed her steps then and started to enjoy the window-shopping around her. Bremerhaven seemed to be as neat as a new pin with washed streets and shopkeepers still busily sweeping out their storefronts.

She passed several bakeries and eating places that were crowded with people not willing to wait until lunch for more calories. At the end of the block, she came upon a square ringed with food wagons like an old-fashioned Western. In this German version, covered wagons were selling fish with the day's catch neatly displayed on trays of ice. Along the line were sausage emporiums interspersed incongruously with wagons displaying fresh flower arrangements.

Paige lingered for a few minutes, and then made for a bank in the next block to cash some travelers' checks. With typical German efficiency, she was ushered out of the building later, clutching considerably fewer marks than she'd thought possible, thanks to the exchange rate and some unusual charges apparently explained in German on her bank receipt.

She sat down on a bench along the pedestrian mall, trying to divide her money to cover lunch, shopping, and then a cab ride back to the dock. When she later walked down to the taxi rank and found out the going rate back to the ship, she gave silent thanks to Heinrich for her transportation into town, or she would have gone without lunch altogether. Fortunately there wasn't much in the stores to tempt her, except for some German cologne in a shop that accepted a credit card. By then, even her coffee had worn off, and she walked back to the place where she'd seen the outdoor food wagons. Another quick currency calculation showed that she could manage a waffle from a nearby stand if she didn't order whipped cream or strawberries atop it.

That snack gave her the energy to start walking again, and this time she followed the corner signs on the *FuBgangerzone* to the ship museum, which Heinrich had told her was one of the places that visitors must see. After crossing a pedestrian bridge, she looked down on a small harbor where a half-dozen different kinds of ships were anchored in the picturesque setting. She saw visitors crossing the boarding platforms to the old-time sailing vessels and various naval ships of World War II vintage, before noticing what was obviously a ticket booth at the end of the walkway. "Damn," she muttered under her breath, wondering whether to pay the entrance fee and then cash another traveler's check, or give up on her sightseeing.

There was a World War II German submarine tied up closest to where she was standing, and she decided at least to go over and see how much the admission fee was. After years of watching U-boats on the late movie, it would be fun to really go aboard one.

She was standing near the ticket booth for the sub and trying another currency calculation in her head, when a familiar voice sounded behind her.

"Having trouble deciding which one to go aboard?" John asked, taking her elbow and moving her aside so that another couple could go pay their admission.

Paige stared up at him in surprise and tried to think of the right answer. "I didn't expect to see you here," she said finally.

"I don't know why not. You'll probably find most of the freighter's crew here sometime during the afternoon. It's called a busman's holiday," he added with a slight smile. "I'm glad to see that you took time off from the malls to come down, too."

By then, Paige realized that she had to find a legitimate reason for not going aboard the sub, so that she could salvage her dwindling German money supply. "I was just giving the place a quick look before I catch a cab back to the ship."

He frowned and glanced at his watch. "What's the hurry? Nothing will be happening there for a while, and you don't look as if you've exhausted the stores yet."

Paige was aware that her single small shopping bag containing a bottle of cologne made it useless to deny his comment. "It's not that," she said, trying to think of another escape. "Actually I'm not keen on touring any more ships."

"You'll find a German U-boat considerably different from the Eccles Line," he said, putting a firm hand in the middle of her back and steering her toward the ticket booth. "This is part of your education if nothing else. Surely you can allow fifteen minutes for that." He pulled up suddenly to direct a quelling glance her way. "Unless you've got your new German chum hanging around waiting for you. The one who was draped over you this morning."

"He wasn't 'draped' at all," she retorted, delighted that Heinrich had served a small purpose other than getting her into the city.

"Okay—so he wasn't draped. Is he the reason you're in such a hurry?"

Paige felt a moment's indecision, and then realized that she'd blown a perfectly good excuse when she saw his grim expression lighten as she admitted, "No. He just drove me into town and bought me a cup of coffee. Although I fail to see what business it is of yours."

"You're probably right. Put it down to a nosy nature. You were lucky this time," he said, starting her toward the ticket booth again. "I wouldn't push it though. There are some tough customers hanging around these docks."

"I am perfectly capable of handling my own life—" she started and then broke off to insist, "I'll get my ticket," as he collected two tickets from the elderly man in the booth after shoving some marks under the wicket.

"Why don't you relax," John said, gesturing her

ahead of him on the walkway to the sub. "Besides, if I buy your ticket, you'll have to listen to me showing off my knowledge of German U-boats."

She gave him an uncertain look. "*Are* you an expert on them?"

He was picking up a brochure and handing a coin to an elderly man by the steps leading down to the submarine. "I will be if you give me time to read one page ahead in this. Otherwise, we'll have to pool our ignorance." Her smile in response gave her face a fleeting beauty that made him suddenly scowl and concentrate on the brochure. "Want to have a look at this?"

"I'll let you tell me all about it." She went down the small flight of stairs and ducked to go inside the sub. "I can see why they didn't want any overweight crew members. Lord, I could have claustrophobia even tied at the dock."

"Umm." He nodded as he scrutinized the wooden paneling in one section. "I'm surprised at that," he said, indicating it. "The Nazi safety engineers must have lost out to an interior decorator."

"Or, maybe Göring had a say in the final design," Paige commented, looking around the close quarters. "I don't think it would be diplomatic to ask any of the people around here. You'll have to read the brochure and see what it says." Then she sobered as they moved on down the U-boat to view the lethal-looking machinery that launched the torpedoes.

"What's bothering you?"

John was apparently keeping her under scrutiny, as well as the sub's interior. Paige chewed on her lower lip before glancing up at him to say,

"It just suddenly came back to me how much devastation and misery the U-boat pack caused in the Atlantic during those years. I realize it's history now, but the families involved will never forget."

"You're right." John took a deep breath. "I don't know about you, but this seems like a hell of a place to be on a great autumn day. Let's get out of here."

Paige nodded and fell in behind him as they made their way past the other visitors to the steps where they'd entered the sub. It wasn't until they were on the catwalk leading back to the central shopping area that she felt the depression from the U-boat disappear. She slowed her steps when they came to a main intersection by the harbor, and wondered how to manage a graceful leave-taking. With the current state of her finances, she couldn't even invite John to share a cup of coffee. And she certainly had no intention of telling him of her plight, for fear he'd think she was asking for a loan.

Meanwhile, he'd shoved his hands in his trouser pockets and was giving her a quizzical look. "I never know what's going through your mind," he said finally. "You've gone from one doom-and-gloom scenario to another in about thirty seconds. If I'm not stepping on Hans's toes or anybody else's, would you like to wander around town before heading back to the ship?"

"That sounds wonderful!" Her response was so fast that he couldn't hide his surprise or the grin that followed it. "Okay, we've got a deal." He took her elbow and steered her across the street. "It sounds as if your social schedule is in the same

shape as mine. By choice, of course." He added
the last when he felt her stiffen at his final words.

Paige wouldn't have broken the newfound peace
between them for anything. She relaxed and confessed, "The only thing I've planned before going
back to the ship is to mail some postcards I've
written. Is it all right if we swing by a post office?"

"Only if we can sit down and have coffee and a
pastry *mit Schlag* afterward."

"It's a deal." Paige didn't attempt to hide the
happiness in her voice. "Lead on—we may need
those calories when we try to find a post office."

At the end of the block, they came abreast of a
restaurant that had a patio with some very satis-
fied-looking customers sitting under umbrella
tables.

"On second thought," John said, pulling up to
survey it before looking inquiringly down at her,
"I could definitely use those calories now. How
about you?"

"Lunch *was* a little thin," Paige admitted. Not
for anything would she have admitted exactly why
it was so thin, but the patio restaurant seemed
like a wonderful place to quell her hunger pangs.

"Then what are we waiting for," John said in a
satisfied tone.

There was an empty table close by the sidewalk,
and Paige sank gratefully into a metal chair that
he pulled out for her. "I must be out of condition,"
she confessed. "It feels wonderful to sit down."

"Cobblestone streets don't help," John said,
looking over a menu that was lying on the table.
"I hope you like sausage—they've got fourteen different kinds of it. What sounds good to you?"

Paige had already located an expresso bar just under the awning of the main restaurant. "I'd love a *café latte* and one of those pastries like the ones they're eating at that table." She nodded to a nearby group where the waiter was unloading a group of desserts that would have had all the dieters in the United States holding their collective heads.

John smiled across the table approvingly. "Thank God! I was afraid you'd just want black coffee or mineral water. Now I can indulge, too, and still be polite."

Paige waited until he'd passed their choices on to a hovering waiter, and watched the man head for the expresso machine before saying, "I didn't know that you spent any time worrying about diplomacy."

John winced visibly at her words. Then he said wryly, "Whatever happened to our truce? It hasn't lasted long enough for the ink to dry on the page."

"Sorry." She gave him a shamefaced grin. "It was just a reflex action. You must admit that our relationship hasn't been worth any trumpet flourishes so far. Although it hasn't been all your fault."

He burst out laughing, bringing a startled look to the waiter, who had just arrived with their steaming coffees. John subsided long enough for them to be placed in front of them and allow the man to depart before saying, "That's one of the most reluctant apologies I've ever heard."

"It wasn't an apology. At least, not really. After all, you weren't a ray of sunshine this morning when Pearl brought our coffee. I got the feeling you were going to be very busy all day."

John rubbed the back of his neck, as if trying to ease a painful muscle. "I guess you have a point. But then you hadn't been on the receiving end of Hans's lectures this past day or two. From the way he talked, you practically have a ring on your finger."

"A what? Oh, heavens—" Her incredulous outburst caught the waiter again—this time as he was putting whipped-cream Napoleons on their table, and it required a quick maneuver from Paige to avoid getting them in her lap. "It's all right," she said hastily, seeing his chagrin. "No harm done." And then when he'd made a hurried departure, she turned to John. "You can stop laughing now, or you'll choke on that coffee."

"I'm sorry," he wiped the corner of his eye with the back of his hand. "For a minute, it looked like a replay of the Three Stooges, only with pastries instead of pie."

"Very funny. But you started the whole thing talking about Hans." She broke off to put some sugar in her coffee, take a tentative sip, and then add another spoonful. "Did he bother to say who was putting the ring on my finger?"

"Oh, yes. He wasn't at all reluctant about that." John was keeping his attention on his first bite of Napoleon so that he didn't miss any of the whipped cream oozing from it.

"Well, for Pete's sake—let me in on the secret," Paige said impatiently.

"His good friend Lucius Smith. Your employer and benefactor, I gather."

Although he kept his voice carefully level, Paige didn't care for the undertone. "I'm not sure what you mean by benefactor. He's the one who okays my pay voucher twice a month so the university can issue a check. He also suggested that I book a round-trip passage on the freighter for my vacation, and said he had a friend on this sailing who'd keep an eye on me." She toyed with a piece of pastry on the edge of her plate before going on. "There was some mention about needing my help on the trip back. If that makes me a scarlet woman—"

He interrupted as her voice trailed off. "That's all?"

"As far as I'm concerned. He's taken me to dinner a few times when we've worked late, but it was the campus cafeteria and, believe me, there are no dark corners or any soft music in that place."

"I'll be damned," John said, frowning.

While there wasn't any obvious change in the crisp, sunny afternoon, Paige distinctly felt the effect of a brisk wind between them, clearing the atmosphere. Her appetite reappeared, and the first bite of her Napoleon tasted wonderful.

"If that's the case, why in the devil was Hans waving me off so strenuously?" Like a terrier hunting for a buried bone, John was reluctant to give up the subject.

"I haven't the foggiest idea." Her comment came after a perceptible pause, and as he shot her a frowning glance, she went on reluctantly, "Lucius sort of fancies himself as an older edition of God's gift to women. And when somebody like that is your boss, it can be a little difficult. It's just possible that he gave Hans an altered version of our relationship."

"So it seems. Hans told me that you were planning a great reunion in London, and there wasn't any mention of research."

Paige put her fork down on the edge of her pastry plate with more care than necessary. "Since my dear employer is staying in a hotel near Russell Square and I have reservations in Sloane Square—it's going to be a little difficult to schedule an orgy."

John laughed and raised his hands in surrender. "Okay, I give up." But as he picked up his coffee cup, he warned, "It sounds as if you might have more trouble convincing your employer, though, when you get to London."

"You might be right." Paige raised her glance to meet his across the table. "Could we forget about him for now? It's a pretty day, and once you ignore how much everything costs in this benighted place, you can enjoy it."

John nodded, and his slow smile appeared. "There is something to be said about not having damp tablecloths and chained-down chairs. We'd better not tell the captain, though, or we won't be allowed back aboard."

From then on, things got even better. Once they'd finished the last bit of pastry and had a second cup of coffee, they wandered back to the street and made their way down the sidewalk toward the post office to mail her postcards.

The small brick building came into view eventually and, a few minutes later they were headed back up the pedestrian mall for the taxi rank that Paige had discovered earlier.

They were so deep in conversation that the youthful shriek of laughter nearby barely penetrated, and it took the sound of pounding feet behind them to make them peer over their shoulders.

There was more laughter from the teenage girl darting toward them, closely pursued by a boyfriend. She was so intent on escaping him that she suddenly dodged and collided with John, losing her balance in the process. He twisted and managed to catch her before she crashed onto the cobblestones as she shrieked again—but this time in fright.

Immediately there was the usual confusion with other pedestrians offering to collect her belongings, which had scattered around them while John got her upright again, brushing aside her thanks and apologies from the young man. At least, Paige's sketchy high-school German thought they were apologies.

John waved them past brusquely with one hand, and they had walked almost half a block before Paige noticed that he was holding his left arm stiffly against his side. She drew up abruptly.

"What's wrong now?" John frowned down at her.

"That's what I want to know." She gestured toward his side. "I think you came out of that fracas considerably worse than the girl. And don't go all macho and stiff upper lip on me."

"Oh, for Lord's sake—I just pulled a muscle when I caught her. It's nothing terminal."

"I didn't say it was." Paige's tone showed that

he wasn't the only one who could sound justifiably annoyed. "Do you want to prove your point by trying the four-minute mile, or shall we head for the taxi rank?" Then, when he muttered something under his breath, she added irritably, "Honestly you have the shortest fuse of any man I've ever met!"

"And ours was probably the shortest peace proclamation on record," he informed her, marching up the middle of the pedestrian mall like a crusader on a quest.

Paige had to practically run to keep up with him, but her depleted wallet forced her to abandon thoughts of going off in a huff and taking a separate cab. That, and the fact that John was still keeping his left arm immobilized against his side. After three blocks in silence, they finally approached the taxi rank. Wishing that she wasn't quite so breathless from trying to keep alongside him, she said, "I suppose it's useless to suggest we stop in a hospital emergency room on the way back to the ship."

"You're right," he said, not slowing his steps.

"Then you'll do it?"

"Hell, no, I meant that it was useless to suggest it."

She pulled up next to the taxi at the head of the queue, and stood back so that the driver could open the door. "The captain wouldn't approve of your attitude."

John merely gestured her in with his right hand, ignoring her comment.

Paige realized it was useless to continue her warnings, but noted that he took considerably

more care than usual when he slid onto the backseat, leaving a substantial distance between them.

After he had successfully gotten across to the
driver that they wanted the container terminal and
settled the amount of the fare, he leaned back in
the corner of the seat and kept his attention
straight ahead.

For one gay, mad moment Paige thought about
introducing a conversation on Bremerhaven's suburban features and then, after another look at
John's stern face, decided it would be a losing
cause.

When they had finally pulled up at the dock
gate, she made a token effort to pay her half of
the fare, which was brushed aside the same way
he'd attend to a bothersome fly. Paige was seeth-
ing by that time, but didn't let it show.

Even when they arrived at the bottom of the
gangway some ten minutes later, she was marching
dutifully and silently beside him. She noted the
only activity was at the bow of the ship, only by
then, the lined-up flatbed trucks were bringing
containers to be put aboard the freighter.

Paige noticed that John was careful to use only
his right hand hanging onto the railing on the
gangway, and his expression was considerably
more drawn than earlier in the day.

She was still trying to decide whether to ask
him if he'd like another cup of coffee as they came
abreast of the dining saloon.

Her hesitation by the heavy glass doors caught
his attention enough for him to say, "I'll see you
later then," over his shoulder as he continued up
the stairs to the next deck.

Paige was left with her mouth open at the bottom, as he disappeared onto the upper deck heading toward the passenger quarters.

So much for her good intentions. So much for hoping he'd say he'd enjoyed their afternoon together. So much for anything, she thought sadly as she walked in the galley for another cup of coffee, which she didn't want!

The next time, she'd take a cruise ship filled with charming men, she told herself, as she yanked down a thick white mug from the metal cabinet. As far as this trip went, she only had another day or so before going ashore in England and the chance to temporarily escape from such an exasperating man. In the meantime, if he wanted to suffer—she'd let him suffer in solitude.

It was especially irritating to acknowledge that suffering alone was exactly what the idiot preferred to do.

Chapter Four

IT WAS CONSIDERABLY later when Paige's feminine pride and determination crumbled into little pieces just like the hard roll on her bread-and-butter plate.

By then, she'd found that dinner aboard was going to be a solitary affair with only the steward, Salvatore, serving as a temporary waiter.

"I lost the toss," he'd told Paige when he'd presented her with a menu that was considerably briefer than usual. "Everybody who isn't on the duty roster is ashore, and since we're sailing two hours earlier than planned—they didn't waste any time leaving the ship."

"The captain, too?"

"He went off in the middle of the afternoon. The mate has the duty, and he's eating on the bridge."

"How about Hans—I mean the chief?"

"I know who you mean," Salvatore said, filling her water glass from the pitcher on the table. "Nobody's getting any closer to him than they have to. Those new parts aren't working right, and it looks as if we'll have to put in for extended repairs in Felixstowe when we get to England."

Paige looked up from the menu in surprise. "Won't that upset the schedule?"

"You said it, miss. That means the front office will be taking the chief apart. They'll claim that his department's maintenance was faulty. And don't quote me—but maybe they're right."

Paige put the menu down and said quietly, "Just some fruit salad, please. And coffee."

"That's a good choice. The chef has some fresh supplies to work with tonight. But what about dessert? I can recommend the apple strudel."

"You've convinced me." Salvatore had taken just a few steps toward the galley before she asked casually, "Oh, by the way—is Mr. Winthrop coming down for dinner?"

Salvatore shrugged and then shook his head. "I don't think so. He didn't say anything about it when I took some towels in his stateroom a little while ago. Maybe he's going ashore again."

"Ummm, could be." Paige made her tone as noncommittal as possible. Then, before Salvatore could disappear around the corner, she said casually, "Would you make that a double order of fruit salad, please? I've been getting hungry in the middle of the night, so I'll take the extra serving up to the refrigerator on our deck."

"You should have told me before," Salvatore said with a concerned look. "I'll check out that refrigerator tonight and make sure there's plenty of food up there."

"Oh, heavens! Don't bother. I'm sure there are plenty of calories around." Paige was sorry she'd mentioned it, since he seemed convinced she was teetering on the edge of malnutrition.

"I'll see," he promised darkly. "But I'll bring the extra fruit for you now in case you get hungry early. Maybe an extra helping of strudel, too."

"Thank you," Paige said meekly. She watched him disappear around the corner, and wondered what she'd do with all that food if John rebuffed her when she pounded on his cabin door. For, no matter what Salvatore reported, she couldn't think that John was in any shape for coming down to dinner, and certainly not to go ashore for the last-minute celebrations. That only left the sixty-four-dollar question: Would he even open his door when she knocked on it?

Fortunately Salvatore was so anxious to get ashore himself, that there weren't any more questions or conversation about the contents of the passengers' refrigerator.

By the time Paige had finished her dinner, he'd left an attractive salad plate covered with plastic and a generous extra serving of strudel on a disposable saucer. She carefully made her way back up the stairway and down the deserted corridors with her burdens. At least she didn't have to worry about the ship's motion sending them flying, she thought thankfully.

There was a stack of messages clipped to the outside of the captain's door, which showed that he, too, was apparently still ashore. The radio operator's door was tightly closed, as was the chief mate's at the other end of the corridor.

She was breathing hard when she reached her cabin after climbing five decks. Once she was safely inside with the food stashed atop the dressing table, she stood and stared at it—wondering what would be the best approach to the man next door.

Perhaps a simple request, she decided. That way, she could scout out the scene and later drop the extra food overboard if need be. The fish in the middle of the Channel wouldn't object to a midnight feast.

She checked her appearance, and then slipped out into the corridor to knock on the door of the suite before she completely lost her nerve.

"Who is it?"

The growled response from inside made her hesitate before finally managing to reply, "It's me or—is it I? Anyhow, I wanted to ask you a favor."

There was a perceptible pause while John evidentally debated the merits of continuing the conversation. Finally he asked reluctantly, "Exactly what kind of a favor?"

Paige was tempted to yell, I'd like to borrow your body for a few minutes, but at that moment the helmsman who was going on duty came stomping up the stairs behind her en route to the bridge. He stared, evidently wondering why she was keeping watch over a closed door, but nodded cheerfully when she managed a smile and, "Good evening."

John must have heard the exchange, and decided it was better to open the door than continue their shouting match. He pulled it slightly ajar, but before he could open his mouth, Paige gave him a bright smile and pushed past him into the living area of the suite. There was just a small lamp turned on at the desk, and, with the curtains pulled over the windows facing the bow, she concluded that her reluctant host hadn't been planning any riotous activities ashore. That decision was strengthened by the sight of a bottle of scotch and a half-full glass next to it.

"Forgive me for sounding inhospitable—" John's sarcastic tones interrupted her survey of the room. "Apparently you wanted something."

Brought back to the present so quickly, Paige's mind went suddenly blank as she tried to remember what reason she'd concocted for her visit. "I— I—" My Lord! she thought desperately, I'm beginning to babble. Evidently John was getting the same idea, because the frown on his tired face deepened as he stared down at her. "I—I wondered if I could borrow some sugar."

He shot a quick glance at the glass of scotch on the desk, clearly wondering if he'd had too much. "You want what?" he asked carefully.

"Sugar," she said almost defiantly. "To go in coffee."

"I know what it goes in, for God's sake."

"Well, then—"

"I don't keep it around." He was back in his terse manner of the afternoon, and she saw that he was keeping his arm down at his side in the same stiff position. Although he'd shed his sweater, he was still dressed in the turtleneck she'd remembered. "You'd better try up on the bridge—they usually have some extra."

"Oh, I can't bother them—not when they're so busy."

"It isn't exactly a hive of activity when we're still tied to the dock," he reminded her. Then, when she showed no inclination to move, he waved a reluctant hand toward the divan, which faced the desk. "Do you want to sit down?"

"Why, thank you." Paige was carefully perched on the edge before his last word came out.

Her action was so transparent that his lips twitched momentarily, but he was back to normal when he walked over to lower himself carefully into the chair in front of the desk. "If you're looking for sugar, I don't imagine you're interested in a glass of scotch," he said, picking up his drink again and rattling the ice cubes.

"No, thanks. I can't stand the stuff."

His eyebrows went up. "Okay, I'll bite. Why the big sugar hunt? Is there a scavenger hunt that I didn't know about, or did the chef go on a health kick?"

She shook her head. "Nothing so drastic. I just wanted it for coffee."

"Well, Salvatore should be able to help you—"

"He's gone ashore." She looked pointedly at the chrome carafe on the back of the desk behind the scotch bottle. "He mentioned that you had some coffee."

He shook his head slightly as if to clear it. "What makes me think that I've missed the first chapter?"

"I can't imagine." Heartened by the fact that he hadn't actually ordered her back into the corridor, she got up to peer into the carafe. "Did he bring a cup and saucer, too?" she asked hopefully.

He merely waved toward the bedroom. "Help yourself. They're still clean. I wasn't in the mood for coffee."

Paige could have told him that she wasn't either,

but it provided a possible excuse for her presence, and it obviously wasn't the time for revealing her real one.

"Do you want me to go and get them?"

She gave him a startled glance as his words finally registered. "Get—oh, the cup and saucer. No, of course not. Be back in a second."

After retrieving the china from his bedside table, she lingered just long enough to see that neither of the spreads on the twin beds had any wrinkles. She walked back out to the lounge with a thoughtful look on her face.

John frowned as she concentrated on pouring the coffee and then watched her settle back on the divan. "Can you stand it without sugar?" he asked when she took the first sip.

"Uh-huh. Black's fine," she answered absently, and then gave him a guilty look as she remembered her original ruse. "Actually, I prefer it with milk and sugar but—"

"Okay—okay." He looked amused for a moment and then settled himself carefully into the desk chair. "I presume you had your reasons."

She nodded, but took another sip of coffee saying, "I think I'd better finish this in case you decide to toss me out once you hear what they are. Have you planned to spend the rest of the night in that turtleneck, and sleep standing up?"

He gave a start of surprise at her words, and then grimaced with pain after the unplanned movement. "What the devil are you talking about?"

"It doesn't take one of the brothers Mayo to diagnose that you either pulled a muscle or cracked a rib on the little maneuver downtown." She took another sip of coffee and stared at him over the rim of the cup. "I'd put my money on the cracked rib. The only time I had one, the doctor said it would get well without any help in six weeks, but I still think you should go and see someone who practices medicine with a license."

"I don't suppose it would do any good if I told you to mind your own damned business."

She looked regretful. " 'Fraid not. I'd simply have to think of another excuse for crashing your party. Besides, my motives are above question. I wondered if you could get out of that turtleneck before you tried to get some sleep."

"And tomorrow, you're going to cut my bacon at breakfast."

The tone of his voice warned her with that one. "Certainly not. If you're as smart as I think you are, you'll order a soft-boiled egg. Although I don't see why you're being so cagey about this. You really couldn't help it."

"That's big of you."

"And I'll excuse your lousy manners because you're having to make the best of an uninvited guest. Meaning me—or is it I?"

"I'll buy you an English grammar in London." He put his empty glass down on the desk with more force than necessary. "I'm sorry—I suppose you mean well. Can I hope that you know when to keep your mouth closed?"

"I was a Girl Scout once—if that helps." After a tiny hesitation, she went on earnestly, "I can keep quiet about lots of things, unless you have a dastardly motive."

"Not dastardly—just self-preservation," he said

wearily. "You know what the rule is on freighters—with no doctor aboard, the captain would be forced to put me ashore here or in England."

"So that you couldn't sue the Eccles Line if something dreadful happened to you on the way back across the Atlantic."

There was a touch of wryness to his voice as he said, "I'd like to think that maybe the Eccles Line was concerned and wanted me to get the proper medical treatment ashore." His expression lightened as he added, "You don't have any relatives who are ambulance chasers, do you? That sounded pretty cynical for somebody your age."

"Oh, for heaven's sake—I'm twenty-four."

"Practically on the edge of senility, and I never noticed."

"Could we possibly get back to the reason for this conversation?"

"You mean borrowing the cup of sugar—okay, put down the crockery. I'll get back to the subject. I'd just prefer that nobody aboard knows about my ailment."

"Well," she chewed uncertainly on her lower lip. "Do you promise to go and see a doctor when we get to Felixstowe?"

"Or London," he agreed casually. "Scout's honor. Boy Scout, if that will convince you."

"Okay." She was observing him through half-closed eyes. "I'll go along with it, but I think you'd better change tactics if you want to convince anybody else."

"What are you talking about?"

"You're going to have to part company with that turtlenecked shirt before we get to Britain, or

Pearl and Salvatore will be suspicious. Especially since you've been looking like a cover from *GQ* for most of the trip." She took special delight in watching a flush go over his tanned face at her observation.

"I did try to take it off," he admitted finally, "but it hurt like the devil. If I had a pair of scissors, I'd cut the damned thing off."

"If you'll let me try, I think we can get you out without any drastic measures."

"Okay—I'd be grateful. I had visions of spending the next week in it." He eyed her with some alarm as she approached. "The right side is fine, but the left—"

"—Is definitely off-limits. I'll remember." He seemed taller than she remembered as she came up beside him, and there was the faintest whiff of a citrus after-shave when she started gathering the body of the turtleneck on his right side. His skin was firm and tanned, and she was trying so hard to avoid contact with it, that she gave a jerk when her knuckles brushed the side of his chest.

John reacted to her sudden movement with a wince of pain. "Ouch! Damn it, I wish you'd stop bouncing around."

"Sorry." She took a deep breath and tried to get her pulse back on an even keel. Compressing her lips firmly, she carefully worked the shirt up to his shoulder and pulled it so he could extricate his right arm. After that, he only needed a small amount of assistance to pull the shirt over his head. When that was accomplished, she happily let him pull it down his injured arm and side.

"Thank God!" he said, forcefully discarding the

shirt and subsiding on the desk chair with a sigh of relief. "I'd like to drive a stake through the thing before I toss it overboard."

"Try that and every environmental group in the English Channel will put shots across our bow," she responded, trying not to be intimidated by the expanse of masculine chest in her view. "For a while I'd suggest a wraparound robe or coat-style pajamas."

"Yes, Mother. Any other suggestions?" Before she could reply, he put in quickly, "I'm sorry. I should be thanking you for getting me out of that straitjacket instead of giving you a bad time. Besides, I'll have to ask you another favor."

"Exactly what did you have in mind?"

"Evidently not what *you* have in mind," he replied, giving her a puzzled look. "Do you dislike the male sex in general or have I been put in a special category?"

"Now you're imagining things. Would you like something to eat? I brought some fruit salad up to my cabin, or Salvatore said he'd put some extra goodies in the refrigerator. You could have a cheese—"

"I wasn't thinking of food," he interrupted when she finally had to draw breath. "Actually, I wondered if you'd mind going ashore with me when we reach Felixstowe?"

She stared at him, mystified by the request. "Not at all. But I hadn't really planned to spend any time there. I promised I'd get the first train up to London."

"Ah, yes. Your professor."

"Not *my* professor. I told you before—I just

work for the man." She put out her hands in a helpless gesture. "I can hardly come all the way to England, and then not even have tea or whatever with my boss."

"The tea's okay," John responded without thinking. "I'm not sure about the whatever." When Paige's lips parted in amazement, he went on hurriedly. "Sorry. Forget that I said that. Anyhow, I wouldn't need to intrude on your social schedule. You see, there's this woman—"

Paige didn't let him finish the sentence. "—And you're giving me a bad time about my perfectly respectable employee-employer relationship."

"Will you just belt up and let me finish?"

From his tone, Paige decided it was best not to argue. "Okay—so there's a woman."

"You don't have to make it sound like a sex ring from the Profumo scandal," he said with asperity. "She's a nice person who works in the Eccles Line office at Felixstowe. I met her there and went out with her a couple times about a year ago. Somehow she got wind that I was coming on this trip and—" he hesitated, obviously trying to find the diplomatic way to explain.

"And you have no desire to further the relationship?"

"Oh, for God's sake—there is no 'relationship.' I took her out twice to dinner. That was it as far as I'm concerned."

"But you're afraid she'll be at the end of the gangway when we tie up?"

He nodded reluctantly. "If I know Fenella— she'll beat the customs officers aboard."

For the first time, Paige allowed herself a sympathetic grin. "And you'd like a red herring to put her off the chase—or something of that sort. Am I right?"

"Something like that." He peered into the carafe. "Sure you don't want some more coffee?"

She shook her head. "Now that we're being honest, I'll admit that I didn't even want the first cup." She hesitated a minute and then asked, "Do you want me to help you into your robe?"

"There's no need. I can certainly manage that unless—" he gave her a thoughtful glance. "You don't have to look so uneasy. It's perfectly okay for a man to be topless."

He made no attempt to hide the amusement in his voice, and Paige reached for the only defense that made sense. "I was just afraid that Hans might come calling again, and I didn't want to have to go through another set of explanations. Especially since you don't want to tell the truth."

His expression sobered suddenly. "You're right about that, and I shouldn't have teased you. I'll get it—" A sudden knocking on the corridor door interrupted his words. "Damn!" he said softly as Paige gave a nervous start. "At the risk of making this sound like a French farce, get in the bathroom and close the door." Then, he added loudly, "Just a minute—I'm coming."

Paige didn't hesitate to follow his order, making a beeline for the bathroom, which separated the lounge from the suite's bedroom, and hastily closed the door behind her.

Almost simultaneously, she heard the door to the corridor being opened and the mumble of masculine voices. She couldn't distinguish the words even though she kept her ear against the metal door.

That almost proved to be her undoing a minute or two later, when John abruptly pulled the door open again and she practically fell into his arms. His sudden grin made her give him an annoyed look. "Okay, so I was listening. What happened?"

"Not much. It was the third mate inviting me up to the bridge. Apparently we're sailing in half an hour, and he thought I might like to meet the port pilot."

"That means you'll have to get dressed properly."

"I know that," he said with some annoyance. "I loused up my ribs, not my head. Besides, I told him I'd pass this time."

"Won't he think that's strange?"

"I can't imagine why. It was just a courtesy gesture, after all." He made his way over to the door leading into the corridor again, and stood there with his hand on the knob. "I appreciate your help."

He didn't say, "Here's your hat—what's your hurry," but there wasn't any doubt that he could dispense with her company, Paige thought. She tried not to show how much his curt dismissal hurt, as she managed to smile and move over to the door herself. "It was no problem. After all, what are neighbors for? Be sure and let me know how I'm to act when we finally reach Felixstowe. You know, whether we're just casual shipmates, or whether I'm to be draped over you on the way down the gangplank, so your Fenella will get the right impression."

"With this rib," he said dryly, "I'm not letting

anybody get very close. You'll have to act as a buffer more than anything else. Don't worry about it—I'll fill you in on the details when I know more about the ship's repair schedule. We may be in England longer than either of us planned."

When Paige got back to her own stateroom a minute or so later, she was still trying to decide if his last pronouncement was meant as a promise or a threat.

One thing sure, she told herself, she wasn't going to lose any sleep over the possibilities.

It was especially annoying, therefore, to find herself still awake three hours later when the freighter was headed westward in the Channel, staring out the darkened window of her cabin and counting navigation lights instead of sheep.

Chapter Five

IT WAS JUST past noon when Paige caught her first glimpse of Felixstowe. The freighter had been fairly close to the English coast for some time and, at the moment, she noticed the ship was practically dead in the water.

She peered over the railing from the passenger deck, hoping that state of affairs was because they were waiting for the harbor pilot to come aboard, and not because they were having still more engine problems.

She cast a concerned glance at the navigation bridge just above, and saw with some relief that the third mate was at that moment strolling out to fix his binoculars on the Felixstowe harbor. Paige turned to follow his glance, and saw a small cabin cruiser leaving the harbor and heading for the *Luella Eccles*. The sound of masculine voices coming from above took her attention to the bridge again, and she discovered that John had joined the mate and was apparently waiting for the arrival of the pilot, as well.

He was wearing a loose-fitting nylon windbreaker over a sport shirt, and certainly looked no worse for wear. Paige had been imagining him wracked with pain since he hadn't appeared at breakfast or the early lunch down in the lounge. Which was all very well, she thought with annoyance, except that if he expected her to act as a buffer to his English girlfriend on their arrival, he'd darned well better make himself known. She wasn't going to play a part without even a glimpse of the script he had in mind.

As if her thoughts had suddenly collided with his wavelength, John glanced down to where she was standing by the rail and gave her a casual wave. His gesture caught the third mate's attention, and he followed suit. Only *he*, Paige noted with even more irritation, managed a pleasant smile and nod.

She turned back to stare out over the calm waters of the Channel, as if intrigued by the large German container ship that was passing close by. After that, she pretended great interest in a sailboat that nosed along the freighter's side, while the crew waved in friendly fashion. All the time Paige was wondering if she'd hear footsteps on the metal stairs leading down from the navigation bridge. She waited a full two minutes longer before letting her glance go casually back to the bridge—only to discover that it was vacant again.

"Damn!" she said under her breath, and then had to pretend that she'd bruised the side of her hand on a metal crosspiece when a crewman appeared, paint and brush at his side.

Paige exchanged a few words with him about the pleasant weather, and managed to confirm that the ship's schedule would be delayed probably three days for final repairs at Felixstowe.

She walked around to the other side of the deck, which gave her an unobstructed view of the English coastline. Gently rolling hills provided many of Felixstowe's residents a splendid view of the Channel. The port town's roads wound around in picturesque fashion, and great clumps of trees showed the typical lush green of a British Isles landscape.

Just then, the muted engine vibration became more pronounced, and she noticed white curls of wake as the freighter moved in toward the shore. As she watched, the small pilot launch accelerated away from the ship and made a graceful circle before heading back to the harbor. Evidently the port pilot had come aboard, and it wouldn't be long until they tied up in Felixstowe.

A firm knock at her cabin door a little later brought her upright from trying to close her overnight case atop the bed. At last, she thought with relief, and then consciously wiped the absurd smile from her face before going over to the door.

If she hadn't taken care to sober up before, she would have then, when she saw Hans's tall form hovering on her threshold.

"Hi!" she managed weakly. "You surprised me. I didn't think they were going to let you out of the bilge for the rest of the trip." And then, noticing his grease-stained khaki coveralls, her tone softened. "You look as if you've really put in some overtime. Did you have any sleep last night?"

He rubbed his face with a weary gesture. "Not much. The company is getting their money's worth from me on this trip. By the way, I brought your passport. The immigration people have already cleared the ship."

She nodded and dropped it on her purse. "Then we can go ashore as soon as we dock?"

"It shouldn't be long." He was staring at her suitcase. "Better ask Salvatore to carry that down to the lounge for you. The customs inspector will come aboard as soon as we tie up. He'll have a few questions, but it shouldn't hold you up for long."

"That sounds easy. I was wondering about our sailing time, so that I can tell the professor when I get to London."

He shrugged, and leaned against the doorjamb as if it were too much effort to remain erect. "Who knows? Leave your London phone number with the Eccles office in Felixstowe, and call them each day to check. I imagine Lucius has already been alerted to the change in plans. You'll be seeing him in London tonight, won't you?"

"I imagine so. I thought I mentioned it earlier."

He rubbed the back of his neck, "Maybe you did. Right now, I'd have trouble remembering my own name." His thin mouth twisted with annoyance. "I'd wanted to get up to London and join the party with you two, but it looks as if that's out now. If things change, though, I'll get in touch. We might manage at least one dinner on a table that doesn't go up and down."

For a man who had spent the better part of his life at sea, Paige thought he sounded more bitter than usual. On the trip across the ocean, she'd gotten accustomed to his generally cynical outlook on life and had tried to ignore it.

"You'd better give me your London telephone

number again," he was saying, as he reached in the pocket of his coveralls and found a pencil stub.

Paige wasn't thrilled with the way he seemed to think that she'd be waiting if he chose to call, but since he was a friend of the professor's, she felt she'd better comply. After she fished her reservation letter out of her purse, she watched him copy the telephone number from the top of the stationery.

"We might be able to go to a show," he told her, stowing the pencil and the telephone number back in his pocket. "Don't count on it, though."

She merely nodded and went over to hold the door ajar once he'd opened it. "Good luck," she said brightly when he hovered on the threshold. And then keeping her voice carefully polite, "I'll give your regards to the professor if you don't make it up to the city."

Hans had barely gotten halfway down the stairs, when the door to the suite was jerked open and John stepped out in the corridor. "That was a touching farewell," he said, watching her start of surprise.

"Do you make a habit of bursting out of the woodwork?" she asked irritably.

"Not usually, but I didn't think it would be safe to let him see us together again. Hans is a fine engineer, but he doesn't handle the lighter side of life very well."

"And you do, I suppose?" Paige heard the sarcastic note in her voice, and wished too late that she'd managed a more pleasant reply. Anyone listening in would have accused her of being just as cynical as the chief engineer.

Apparently the thought had already occurred to

the man who leaned against his doorjamb staring at her. "What's wrong? Did lunch disagree with you?"

If he'd been down in the dining saloon for meals, he wouldn't have had to stand around asking silly questions, Paige decided. "I feel fine, thank you. You'd better tell me what I'm supposed to do when your English girlfriend appears. It won't be long until the ship's tied up."

"I *did* notice." He was sounding annoyed again. "You're certain that you don't mind doing this?"

"Of course not, but I'm not sure that you're being honest with the woman."

"Oh, for God's sake! I'm just trying to dodge another dinner date with her—that's all. It's not some great love affair like Edward and Wallis."

"Okay—I apologize." Paige realized that she'd gone too far again. "Do we meet the woman together, or would you like me to come in later?"

"Hell, I don't know. You're making this sound like planning the Normandy landing."

"Okay—so we keep it casual. Just one more thing, are we shipmates or very good friends?"

His stern mouth quirked. "That's two things." Then, when she started to object, "Let's play it by ear. That way it'll be safer. I'll tell Fenella we have mutual friends at home, so she'll think it's more than a casual shipboard acquaintance. I don't want to hurt her feelings any more than necessary."

"Are you sure you're not reading too much into her interest? I mean, maybe she's gotten engaged or something since you saw her last?"

He shook his head at the possibility. "I wish to hell she had. Unfortunately she sent me a message that made the radio officer's day. He could hardly wait to deliver it, so he could find out what my answer was going to be."

Paige knew better than to ask him what he had replied. All she could do was nod and try not to think about the way he dismissed casual acquaintances.

"I have the feeling that I've lost you somewhere along the way."

John's drawled comment penetrated her thoughts, and she blinked, trying to remember what he'd said before.

Fortunately he put her out of her misery. "I think it would be simplest if we meet in the lounge when the customs people arrive," he said. "I'll bring Fenella if she's aboard by then. Have you arranged for your luggage to be taken down?"

"No. Hans said that Salvatore would take care of it."

"He has more faith in him than I have," John said. "Salvatore is nursing a king-size hangover, thanks to his liking for German beer. Don't worry about it, though—I'll make sure he gets yours when he picks up mine."

"Then you're going to London, too? Or are you just spending time ashore in Felixstowe?" Paige kept her voice carefully casual.

"London—if it's possible with this damned rib," he replied, wincing as he took a deep breath. "And London even if it isn't."

His grin appeared briefly, before he gave a casual salute and disappeared back into his suite.

Paige closed her own door and went over to fasten her suitcase, trying not to dwell on the possibility that even in a city as big as London, their paths might coincide. Her expression was wistful as she acknowledged that spending a night at the theater or taking a stroll on Park Lane with John was infinitely more appealing than sharing it with her employer or Hans. As irritating as the man could be at times, the intervals in between were enough to send her pulse bounding. Which was absurd, she told herself, and went over to stare out her cabin window, trying to concentrate on the containers stacked on the nearby dockside as they entered the English port.

Instead of the tremendous bustle of the Bremerhaven, there was a leisurely tone to the whole scene. The trucks didn't move as fast, and there weren't nearly as many of them. The forklift operators were stopping to chat, and the dockers, waiting to handle the big hawsers when they reached the bollards, were leaning comfortably on a handcart. The thermoses at their feet almost certainly contained tea.

Paige smiled at the thought and decided England was her cup of tea, too. It took the sight of a blond woman standing by the side of a small car on the dock to make her smile slowly fade. The woman was waiting near the men who were going to secure the gangway, and she had an expectant look on her face as her gaze searched the side of the freighter.

It didn't take much imagination to identify just who she was looking for, and when she suddenly smiled and started to wave toward the navigation bridge, Paige knew that she'd sighted John.

Paige left the window then and retreated to the

center of her stateroom, unwilling to watch any more. For an instant, she wondered why John was so reluctant to pursue the acquaintance; the woman was attractive and nicely dressed in a heather-shaded tweed suit. It was unfortunate that the short hemline of her skirt revealed a pair of legs that were a little too sturdy to rate any whistles. Even so, that was hardly enough of a failing to make a man start running the other way. Paige shook her head as she thought about it, and then put her mind to other things, when there was a knock on her door and Salvatore's voice proclaimed that he'd arrived to carry her case down to the lounge for customs inspection.

Paige forced herself to wait another fifteen minutes in her cabin before throwing her raincoat over her arm and taking a last look around the stateroom. A search to make sure that her passport and travelers' checks were in her purse was the final safeguard, and then she let herself out into the hallway.

The corridors were still deserted, but she could hear conversation behind the outer door of the captain's cabin, and presumed that the port official-dom had arrived for their refreshments. She moved on quickly, not wanting to be included in any of the hospitality overtures. One more deck down brought her to the glass doors of the lounge, and a hasty glance showed that the main players of the drama were just inside.

Paige took a deep breath and pulled open the heavy door. John turned around to greet her with a broad smile. "I thought you were never coming, darling," he said, as he put a possessive arm around her shoulders. "I want you to meet Fenella Parsons—an old friend of mine. Fenella, this is Paige. Paige Collins," he added.

"How do you do, I'm happy to know you, Fenella," Paige said pleasantly. Then raising her glance to meet John's, she added, "I hope you told Fenella how nice it was for England to greet us with sunshine and a beautiful day."

The Englishwoman looked as if she were having trouble keeping her fixed smile in place. "Yes, indeed," she said. "John has been going on and on about the weather."

There wasn't any doubt that a discussion about the weather wasn't what she had come to hear, and Paige felt a moment's sympathy for her. "Well, I suppose it's because we hit such a storm just before we got in the Channel," she said, trying for a diplomatic touch. Then, looking around the deserted lounge, she asked, "Have the customs people arrived? I don't see my suitcase anywhere."

"It's already down the gangway, darling," John said. "They came aboard when Fenella did and made short work of things. So if you're ready to go ashore, there should be a taxi waiting for us. The captain arranged it." His tone turned brisk as his glance rested momentarily on the Englishwoman. "I suppose you still have some paperwork to finish before you go back to the office."

Fenella took the easy way out. "Yes, of course. This delay has made all of us put in extra time. I'm sorry that you called a taxi, though, I could have ferried you back uptown."

"We couldn't take a chance," John told her. "Not

if we want to make connections with the London train."

The English girl couldn't hide her dismay at his remark. "Aren't you staying in Felixstowe during the layover?"

"Sorry, not this time. We're hoping to take in some theater in London if we can get tickets."

"But where are you staying?" Fenella asked, desperation in her tone.

"What's the name of your club in Sloane Square?" John asked Paige. "I keep forgetting."

Probably because it's the first time he even thought of it, Paige decided, sparing a moment of sympathy for Fenella, who was clearly stricken by his news. Even so, it was best to put an end to her hopes. "The Herald Club, dear," Paige said, managing a fond glance at John. "I'm beginning to think you have a mind like a sieve."

"Only when I'm around you," he replied, following her lead. "Now I think we'd better go ashore. Fenella, it was very nice of you to come down as the welcoming committee. I'm just sorry that time is so short this trip."

"That's quite all right." Fenella straightened her shoulders and flashed a smile that didn't reach her eyes. "Don't forget to ring us up every day in case there's a change of sailing time. If you don't have my number, Miss Collins—I'm sure John does."

It was a weak attempt to regain her feminine pride, and Paige gave her an *A* for effort. She smiled and said, "Thanks—we'll manage. It was nice meeting you."

"Come on, darling." John urged her from where he was holding the lounge door open with his good arm. "Time's a-wasting. See you, Fenella. Give my best to the fellows in the office here."

A taut silence reigned as they went down another flight of stairs and finally out onto the deck. After maneuvering the steep gangway, they had barely set foot on the dock before a piercing whistle sounded. Paige looked back to the ship to see both Salvatore and Pearl cheerfully waving them off. She grinned in response, and followed John to a nondescript beige car with a peeling taxi sign on the door. The middle-aged driver gave her a casual salute, before he opened the trunk of the car and then went over to the foot of the gangway to retrieve their bags.

John had opened the car door, and Paige decided it was simpler to get in before she started asking questions rather than hold an inquisition on the pier. Especially if Fenella was watching from the window of the lounge.

John slid carefully onto the backseat beside her, and the driver settled behind the steering wheel. "Where to, guv?"

"The railroad station, please," John said calmly.

"Righto." The car engine sounded asthmatic, but the driver seemed to accept it as the norm, and turned past a big container handler that was being moved along the tracks to start the unloading process, before accelerating past blocks of stacked containers toward the terminal gate. He came to a token halt there, long enough for the guard to wave him past, and finally turned onto a two-lane highway.

John glanced ahead of them and then turned to

Paige. "Okay, spit it out," he said in a resigned tone. "You look as if you're about to explode."

"Just a little confused," she said, keeping her voice pitched low when the driver appeared fully as interested in them as he was with the traffic. "I didn't know you were going to London today."

"You didn't ask."

Paige could have told him that he hadn't been close enough in the last day or so to ask anything. Instead she plunged on, "And why did you let that woman think that you were staying at the club with me?"

"Because I am. Fenella should learn that a man likes to think he's doing the running. At least she can't miss that we have something going now."

"Something going!" Paige's voice went up in an outraged squeak. Then, catching the driver's intrigued glance in the rearview mirror, she made an effort to regain her composure. "First of all," she told John through clenched teeth, "you are *not* staying with me."

"Perhaps not in the same room," he said calmly, "but I am staying at the same club. The captain got the reservation for me. He belongs to a club in New Orleans that has reciprocal privileges, and it was easier for me than trying to find a hotel room in London at the last minute. Apparently there's an American Bar Convention or something going on. If you haven't confirmed your reservation, I'll be glad to share with you."

"Very funny." Paige couldn't tell exactly how she felt. He'd made a hash of her accusations but, in place of anger, she was feeling strangely expectant over sharing the same roof in London.

Just then, the cab started up a winding narrow street that led to the top of the hill and the town center. She took a minute to admire the view over the Channel to her right. A sailboat regatta was providing color near the shore, while out in the shipping lanes there was a steady stream of freighters and smaller workboats mainly headed for the Continent.

John was following her glance. "Not a bad view, is it? Probably that's why so many Englishmen decide to retire in this part of the world."

"You're right about that, guv." The driver must have been keeping close tabs on their conversation. "It's easy to get to Ipswich for shopping, or the ladies can save their money and have a day in London. Not that you have to, though. I can find everything I need on the High Street." He gestured toward a busy pedestrian mall before turning off to a one-way street close by. Then, seeing John pull a train schedule from his coat pocket, he went on, "Don't worry. You'll be at the station with a bit of time to spare."

He was right about that, pulling up at a curb alongside a small covered area by some double tracks, just as a three-car minitrain came slowly down toward the end of the line.

"I'll help you with your bags," the driver said, evidently aware the John was favoring one arm. A few minutes later, after depositing them inside a dusty coach, where it looked as if they'd be the only passengers, he bestowed a pleased smile when he saw the tip that John pressed into his hand. "Thanks very much. I'll probably see you when you get back. We don't have many taxis to choose from in this town," he said, and slammed the door of the coach behind him.

Paige found herself smiling at the man's confession, and turned to survey the railway car where the velour seats looked as if they'd been installed in Victorian times. She carefully folded her raincoat over one across the aisle before settling down beside John. "I didn't know that British Rail was in such sad shape," she said. And then, "What are you looking at?"

"I'll be damned," he said, staring toward the curb where their taxi was just pulling away.

Paige leaned around to discover what fascinated him. "I don't see anything except a bunch of parked cars."

"You don't—" he broke off as the train gave a jolt and started up. "Well, there's no use taking chances."

And with that pronouncement, he put a possessive arm around Paige's shoulders and bent over to give her a lingering kiss.

She was so astonished to find his firm mouth on hers that, after the briefest hesitation, she let her body relax against him. That made him draw a painful breath, and he brought his head up with a muttered, "Oh, hell!"

Paige shot up straight, flushed with embarrassment and found herself eye-to-eye with the Brit Rail conductor, who wore a navy blue sweater above shiny work pants as his only badge of officialdom, except for a ticket punch in his hand. His expression showed he wasn't keen on foreigners, especially foreigners caught necking on his coach in broad daylight.

"I suppose you want our tickets," Paige said, aware that her cheeks were burning.

"That's the idea, miss."

"I have a pass," she said, finding herself all thumbs as she started to paw through her bag. From the corner of her eye, she saw that John already had his pass out and was handing it to the conductor. His unruffled expression showed that being interrupted in the middle of a kiss clearly didn't bother him.

"You know, sir, that you'll need to transfer to the London train in Ipswich fifteen minutes from now," the conductor was saying. "There won't be time for validating passes there, so you'd best do it aboard the Inter-City."

"Right. Thanks very much," John said, as he took the paper back and stowed it away in his coat pocket.

Paige had found her own pass by that time and handed it over for the requisite punch, hoping that she looked equally calm and collected.

The conductor gave her pass back without comment, merely bestowing an unsmiling nod before heading toward the front coach of the train where he sat down beside the motorman.

"I think you've just been branded as a scarlet woman," John said as he watched Paige put the Brit Rail pass in the side of her purse.

"After hearing that groan of yours, he probably thought that I'd decided to have you for tea." Paige made no attempt to hide her annoyance. "What came over you, for Pete's sake?"

"You hit my rib—"

"I *know* that," she interrupted. "And I'm sorry.

But what brought forth your sudden outburst of affection? Do dusty railroad coaches turn you on? Or maybe it's the shock of being on dry land."

"Or maybe finding a beautiful redhead by my side."

That time, it was Paige who drew a sharp breath at his casual comment.

Before she could savor it, he punctured her sudden hopes. "Actually, I thought I saw Fenella drive up just as the train was pulling out. It seemed like a good idea to solidify our story, so that she isn't tempted to trail us to London."

Paige put her nose against the dusty window and tried to check Fenella's presence, but all she could see were buildings disappearing as the train rattled around a curve.

"Now you've a smudge on your nose," John said, giving her a critical look.

"Oh, Lord." She started rooting in her purse for something to repair the damage.

"Here, let me," he said producing a folded linen handkerchief. "We'll be in London before you find yours. Hold still."

She obeyed reluctantly, even to sticking out her tongue when moisture was needed for the cleaning process.

"Okay—you're presentable again. God knows what the conductor would think if you added a dirty face to your already tarnished reputation."

"Very funny. Especially since it was all your fault. And I'm not a redhead," she protested, going back to his earlier remark.

"You are when you're sitting in the sun," he

observed. "And you certainly have the temper of one."

"Only when I'm around you—" Paige broke off, realizing that she was merely confirming his words. "Never mind. I guess there was no harm done."

"Now you're being sensible. There's no need to make a federal case out of a simple kiss. I certainly wouldn't pick a lousy Brit Rail commuter train for anything more."

"That's reassuring. Besides, with that cracked rib, you haven't a chance against a sharp elbow."

His smile turned wintry. "How true."

Paige could tell that she wasn't going to win any popularity contests if she continued on that theme. She let out a small sigh and shifted on the hard train seat. "I suppose you'll take my head off if I ask what you're going to do about it."

"About what?"

"The alleged cracked rib," she said patiently. "I thought you were going to see a doctor in Felixstowe."

He stirred uneasily. "I changed my mind. But I do have the address of one in Harley Street. I had to tell the captain that I was suffering from indigestion or the company representative would have met me at the bottom of the gangway when I attempted to go back aboard."

She stared at him, puzzled. "Is it so important that you return on the *Luella Eccles*? You could probably get space on a later sailing."

"I'm well aware of that." His tone showed that he didn't plan to continue discussing that topic either. Her crestfallen expression apparently made him soften because he added, "Forget it. I'm betting the man in Harley Street puts me back on the street again as soon as he looks at the X ray and collects his bill." He leaned forward to stare out the train window where the sprinkling of cottages near the track had suddenly become solid suburban residential blocks. "We're coming into Ipswich. Don't drag your feet when we get on the platform. There's only about five minutes until the Inter-City to London arrives. Usually it comes in on the next track, but we'll really have to move if the stationmaster has changed his mind this month."

"I'm glad that you know the score," she said, rubbing the glass of the window beside her so that she could get a better view of the bustling English city they were entering. "You must have done this before."

"Umm."

He was intent on checking that their bags were close to the coach door for a hasty departure, and missed the look of frustration that passed over her face. The man should be in the CIA for all the information that he divulged. Aside from the fact that he was unmarried, wanted out of Fenella's orbit, and apparently had his own teeth, he was still shrouded in mystery.

"What's the matter now?" he queried as the train started to slow down for the main Ipswich station.

She looked up, startled. "What do you mean?"

"You suddenly looked as if you were in pain. Maybe we should make that Harley Street appointment for two."

Paige got up carefully as the engineer applied the train's brakes with more vigor than skill. "The diagnosis will be assault with a deadly weapon if you keep asking me silly questions. Lead on, Horatio. The conductor's coming this way, and he looks capable of throwing us off if we don't make it on our own."

Contrary to her fears, the conductor had had a change of heart and politely told them that the Inter-City would be along on the neighboring track in exactly four minutes, even showing them where they should be standing to board the first-class coaches to London.

After that, it was Brit Rail at its best—which Paige found wasn't to be sneezed at. The comfortable seats were clean, and the roadbed was unbelievably smooth despite the high speed as they left the coast behind and headed toward London. For the first time, Paige realized that she was really in England, and the rolling fields on either side of the train confirmed it.

John evidently was aware of her preoccupation, because he sat quietly across from her, alternately reading the paperback he'd pulled from the side of his bag and checking out the scenery himself. After the conductor had checked their passes and advised to get them properly validated at Liverpool Street Station while in London, John put his book away.

"I swore I wasn't going to weaken," he said ruefully, after noting a passenger going down the aisle carrying coffee and a sandwich, "but the smell of that coffee did it. We could have something standing up at the snack bar, but it looks easier to make use of the facilities here." He indicated the narrow Formica table between their seats.

Paige nodded, putting a detaining hand on his arm when he started to get up. "I don't have any Harley Street credentials, but I think you'd better let me do the delivery service. All you need is to be carrying hot coffee when we hit a curve, and you'll end up either with second-degree burns or another broken rib." She got to her feet, managing to hang onto the back of the seat as the train slowed for one of its few stops. "Black coffee and something sweet or a sandwich?"

John settled back reluctantly in his seat, but reached in his pocket and brought out a five-pound note, which he tucked in the top of her purse. "You deliver—I buy. And cookies will be fine, just so they're not digestive biscuits. I draw the line there."

Paige was tempted to put his money back on the table, and then decided she was being silly. John must have read her expression correctly again, because he just nodded and said, "Cut along while the train's stopped. You'll have an easier trip between cars."

Fortunately the snack bar was only three cars away, and there were only a few people queued up to be served. Paige got the coffee and two packages of English biscuits without trouble. She made her way carefully back to her seat, giving thanks for the lids on the paper coffee cups every time the train rattled around on the roadbed. John had cleared off the table so she could deposit the carrier tray between them.

"As advertised," she said, sitting down and handing him the change from his note. "I can't guarantee the quality of the coffee." She was gesturing toward his cup as she spoke. "Probably we'd have been smarter to order tea."

"I haven't been in England that long," John said, only grimacing slightly as he took his first swallow, "although I might change my mind pretty fast after this."

"Try a cookie," she said, pushing a package across. "There's nothing like a few calories to help the cause along."

They ate in silence after that, but it wasn't a strained one, Paige was glad to note. In fact, the atmosphere seemed pleasant enough that she risked asking, "Are you going to check in at the club right after you arrive, or will you go to Harley Street first?"

John sounded resigned as he replied, "Hell! I suppose I'd better get to Harley Street."

"You won't want to carry a bag around town with you," she pointed out. "What I mean is— you'd do better to put me in a taxi with the luggage. If I remember, there's a doorman at the club who can take over from there. I'll just tell the desk clerk that you'll be along later to register and collect it." She allowed herself a teasing grin, "If I didn't know better, I'd think you'd planned the whole thing this way."

John raked her with a thoughtful glance. "Next you'll be accusing me of taking advantage of free labor. Maybe I'd be better off to just carry the bag."

She shook her head. "No way. Besides, who said my labor is free? I plan to get a meal out of this somehow while we're in London. Providing our schedules mesh, of course." She managed the last in a light tone, so that he wouldn't think she was trying Fenella's tactics.

"Of course." There was just enough amusement in his reply to make Paige give him a suspicious glance. It was ignored as he gestured toward the window when the train lowered speed. "We'll be in the station soon. There was a big construction project going on the last time I was here, so it's a good thing you're wearing walking shoes. The closest taxi rank is practically in Southampton."

The next forty-five minutes passed in a blur, as they arrived in the busy station and threaded their way through the crowds of people hurrying down the concourses to their trains. Paige gave silent thanks that she only had one bag to carry, since carts were evidently about to join condors as an endangered species. She saw John wince once as a commuter brushed into him, but she didn't comment on it, merely trying to keep up with his long steps as they followed the overhead signs to the Brit Rail pass validations window and then to the taxi rank.

A few minutes later when they reached the head of the queue and a cab drew up in front of them, John took over stowing the bags before waving her inside. He then handed the driver some money as he told him her destination. "If there isn't a doorman on duty at the Herald Club, I'd appreciate it if you'd help the lady with the luggage."

The driver, who had been looking at the denomination of the note in his hand, gave him a respectful salute. "Righto, guv. I'll take care of it."

John nodded his thanks and turned back to Paige saying, "I'll see you later. If you go out, leave a message for me," before slamming the cab door.

Paige didn't have a chance to reply. She had to snatch a look through the back window of the cab, and watch him get into the next taxi, which was just then pulling up as her driver accelerated out into the busy street. Even a modern, liberated woman could appreciate a man trying to smooth her way, she decided. Having to wrestle with two bags wasn't an insurmountable task, but even so—Paige started to smile as she thought about it.

The traffic in London seemed to have doubled since the last time she'd been there, and even though the cabbie tried all the shortcuts and went through roundabouts like a rally driver, it took a considerable time for the journey from Liverpool Street station to Sloane Square.

It turned out that John had been right again when the driver stopped under the faded canopy of the club a few minutes later. There wasn't any sign of a doorman, and Paige was relieved to see the cabbie cheerfully hoist both bags to take them into the entrance hall. Paige followed on his heels, wondering if she should be fumbling for an extra tip. As an elderly porter materialized from a straight-back chair near the reception desk to take charge of the luggage, the driver turned back to the door. He didn't even hesitate, giving Paige a casual farewell salute as he got back in his cab.

Another problem solved, Paige thought as she readjusted the shoulder strap of her purse and went over to address a person who looked more like a corporation president than a desk clerk. "Good afternoon," she said when he deigned to acknowledge her presence. "I'm Paige Collins. You should have a reservation for me. Oh, and before I forget, Mr. Winthrop will be here shortly. He sent his luggage along with me."

At the mention of John's name, the clerk's expression underwent a considerable change, becoming almost welcoming as he reached for a registration card. "Of course, Miss Collins. Both your room and Mr. Winthrop's are ready. They have a nice view, so you should be pleased with them. We're always happy to accommodate the Eccles Line any way we can. Gregory." A snap of his fingers brought the elderly porter to his feet again. "Take Miss Collins to 415 and Mr. Winthrop's luggage to 417. Now, if I could see your passport, Miss Collins—just a formality, of course."

Paige handed it over without comment so that he could note the number, wondering if she would have been put in a garret if she hadn't appeared under the aegis of the Eccles Line. Even indirectly.

"Splendid." The clerk handed her passport back and went on to say, "If you plan to have dinner in the dining room, you'll need to make a reservation."

"Thank you. I think I'll wait a bit before I make up my mind." Then, as she started to walk away, another thought struck her and she turned back. "I meant to ask if there were any messages or mail for me."

"Around the corner." He gestured toward the other end of the counter where a woman was manning an old-fashioned switchboard under some boxes that obviously held mail for the club's guests.

She shot an apologetic look over her shoulder

toward the porter, who had subsided in his chair once again rather than stand by the small elevator. When she reached the telephone operator, she had to wait while the gray-haired woman handled a complaint from someone who evidently wanted more heat in the room. The woman promised to dispatch a small heater as soon as she could locate a maintenance man, and looked up with a harried expression.

"I'm Paige Collins," she began only to have the woman cut in.

"—I'm so glad," she said, thumbing through a stack of messages in front of her. "I was afraid I'd be off duty before you checked in, and this was going to be difficult to explain in a note, especially since I promised Professor—" her voice trailed off as she consulted the memo she wanted, "Professor Smith. L-u-c-i-u-s Smith," she went on, giving the name a British pronunciation. "You do know who I mean?" she asked then anxiously.

"Yes, indeed, I work for him." Paige said, unaware that she was hanging onto the marble counter so hard that her knuckles were white. "Is something wrong?"

The woman looked up, puzzled. "I shouldn't think so. He sounded perfectly all right to me. He just mentioned he was making an unexpected trip north—something about Scotland, I believe. Anyhow, he didn't think that he'd be able to meet you in London." The woman was having trouble deciphering her notes on the piece of paper. "You're to go ahead with the research he'd ordered, and he'll try to meet you on the ship." She looked up again. "He didn't say which ship."

"I know which ship," Paige said, frowning. "That was all?"

"There was something about luggage. Oh, yes," she said reading along the margin. "He left a piece here at the club and wants you to take it on board for him. So that he wouldn't have to bother with it when he's traveling around."

That sounded like Lucius, Paige thought with resignation. He didn't ever believe in doing something himself if he could find an assistant to take over the work for him.

"Did I miss something?" The woman was looking at her anxiously.

Paige shook her head again. "I don't think so. Where is the professor's bag?"

"In the storage room, I should think."

"Right." Paige sighed, still trying to assimilate this latest change of plans. "He didn't leave a number where he could be reached, did he?"

"Not to me." The woman's expression was helpful. "Perhaps he'll ring you while you're staying with us."

"Perhaps." He would if he were acting normally, Paige thought as she stood there frowning. Usually she could have set her watch by Lucius Smith's daily movements. Since the man didn't like changes of any kind, the message he'd left was really out of character.

"Was there anything else, miss?" The telephone operator wasn't tapping her fingers, but she clearly wasn't disposed to linger. Especially with the reservations clerk sending a fierce look her way.

"No—no, thank you very much. I'll be up in my room if there are any calls," Paige said, taking the hint and marching back toward the elevator where the porter was still hovering by the luggage.

When she was finally steered to room 415, she was amused to find that the "nice view" was a bird's-eye scene of busy Sloane Street where red double-deck buses and cars went by in a steady stream. It didn't matter because the room was pleasant with twin beds and an adjoining bath. The trimmings were mainly chintz, and the decorator must have liked red roses because there were literally yards of them on the drapes and spreads. Paige was still surveying the swag over the window when the nearby door from the adjoining room opened abruptly. She turned, startled, to find the elderly porter beaming at her.

"I've left the gentleman's bag in here, miss. You can lock this connecting door if you want."

He left it wide open, but Paige stayed immobile until she heard the hall door close and then went quickly over to shut it. Adjoining rooms was one thing, but adjoining rooms with an open door might send John out into the night looking for another hotel. Especially after Fenella and his comment about men preferring to do the running.

Paige gave herself a mental poke then. John wasn't the only one who should prefer a closed door. Just because they'd shared a bed during the storm, didn't mean she hoped for a romantic interval once they set foot on land. She went into the white-tiled bath at that point to survey her reflection in the mirror, deciding that not only was she an awful liar, she was an untidy one to boot.

She wandered back into the bedroom after hanging her raincoat in the closet and looked out the window, trying to decide what to do next. Being in London was like being loose in a candy store, but that rose-covered spread on the nearest bed was inviting, too. Perhaps it would be smart to rest just for a few minutes in case Lucius decided to call or John arrived with a possible invitation to dinner.

The bed was comfortable and seemed even better than usual, because it didn't go up and down at regular intervals as the sidewalks still did. She knew the sensation would soon wear off, but being horizontal was appealing in the meantime. Her eyelids drooped as she thought about the professor's message. Perhaps he'd stay up north and miss connecting for the return voyage of the freighter. She should be disturbed at the prospect, she told herself, but her lips were curved in a smile as she fell sound asleep.

A knock on the hall door brought her upright and wide-awake later on. "Just a minute," she called as, yawning, she swung her legs to the floor and staggered to the door.

"I was just about to send down for a passkey," John said, as he pushed it wide open as soon as she'd turned the knob. "You really should put on the chain when you're staying in a hotel."

Paige was in the middle of another yawn, but felt she had a couple of points in her defense. "I know you're right, but the only two men I've seen here so far are the desk clerk and the porter. I doubt if the desk clerk would dally with anybody lower than royalty, and the porter needed help to get over the threshold. Lord knows how he makes it onto his bed every night." She glanced at her watch then and gasped, "Heavens! I've wasted over three hours sleeping. It's dinnertime."

"That's why I'm here," John said dryly. "Do you think we might discuss it in your room instead of the middle of the hall?"

"Sorry." She gestured him in and closed the door. "I'm still groggy, I guess. How did your Harley Street visit go?"

"I'll live. It's just a cracked rib, and I got the usual lecture about taking it easy." A rare grin crossed his features. "I'm like you, though. If the doctor thinks I plan to waste any time taking to my bed while I'm here, he's crazy."

"You *do* plan to eat, however," Paige said, smiling in response.

He nodded. "Preferably with company. I glanced into that dining room downstairs, and it seems a little staid for uncouth Americans. The waitresses were the same vintage as the porter, and anything less than five courses could count as fast food."

"Is there an alternative?"

"Well, there's an Italian restaurant a couple blocks down. After I registered, I decided to scout out the neighborhood. I thought you were probably out shopping or something. It wasn't until I came back that the porter said you were still in the club. I didn't even consider you might be taking a nap."

"Don't put it on your list of 'possibles' from here on out," she told him. "I don't plan to waste any more time in bed—just like you," she added mischievously.

While she didn't intend a double meaning, she could feel a sudden warmth in her cheeks as he gazed at her with patent amusement. "It might be interesting to see if you could be made to change your mind," he said finally, before looking at his watch. "If we're going to make sure of getting dinner, we'd better go. Some of these neighborhood eating places keep limited hours. Of course, we could always take a cab to Piccadilly."

"I can be ready in a hurry," Paige assured him.

"Okay, I'll wait in my room," he said, starting for the hall again.

"That's the long way 'round," Paige said opening the connecting door. "This is more convenient."

"So it is." He paused halfway through to give her an amused glance. "You don't have to lock it unless you're afraid that I might walk in my sleep."

Her look was just as direct. "Is sleepwalking a habit with you?"

"Hardly. I prefer to be wide-awake. So that everybody concerned knows exactly what's going on."

With that, he closed the door firmly behind him. Paige took a moment to stare at it in bemused fashion. How strange to be holding a conversation that had absolutely nothing to do with the subject in both their minds. However, it was best not to dwell on it just then. If John had any thoughts about a hasty affair, he'd have to learn that convenience wasn't the operative word as far as she was concerned.

Acknowledging that brought an unhappy cast to her features. For the first time, she was forced to admit that the bossy, irritable, and thoroughly annoying man in the next room held an irresistible fascination for her. Which made no sense at all, she told herself. She'd probably hit him over the head with a frying pan before a week had passed, or he'd celebrate the occasion by joining the French Foreign Legion.

The way he'd disposed of Fenella showed what he thought of short liaisons—Lord knows what he'd do at the prospect of a long one!

"Are you about ready?"

His impatient question from the other side of the door brought Paige back to the present in a hurry. "Give me a couple minutes more," she called as she dove into her suitcase for an off-white knit skirt that didn't wrinkle and a sweater with inserts of angora, which was both flattering and comfortable to complete the outfit.

It was probably closer to five minutes than two when she knocked and announced that she was finally ready.

John had the connecting door open before she'd finished speaking. For an instant he stared at her with that unrevealing expression that he seemed to have perfected. Paige started to wonder if there were a run in her hose or some other flaw when he said, "That's quite a transformation. You look too good for a neighborhood bistro."

She smiled, almost light-headed in relief. "I'm glad you like it, because you'll see variations of this outfit at breakfast, lunch, and dinner while we're here. I really packed lightly." Her glance roamed over his gray houndstooth sport coat and cashmere vest. There was a white oxford-cloth shirt, as well, but it was obvious that he was choosing clothes that he could handle with the cracked rib.

"Do I pass?"

His amused tone made her realize that she'd been staring longer than necessary. She wanted to confess that she thought he looked great, but just nodded and made a production out of checking the contents of her purse.

They took the wheezing elevator to the first floor, passing the reception desk and the snoozing porter on their way out.

"It's only a couple blocks down here," John said, gesturing to the right as they reached Sloane Street. "Do you mind walking?"

"I'm all set." Paige stuck out her foot to show a neat beige pump with a low heel. "Lead on."

By then, darkness had settled over the neighborhood and the crowded sidewalks were a thing of the past. They only passed a few strolling couples as they made their way down the block, but the street traffic was still steady. Not the gridlock numbers that Paige had noted earlier, but still enough that crossing the street could have been hazardous to their health. Especially since she looked the wrong way as she stepped off the curb, and John had to pull her quickly back as a car sped past.

"Oh, Lord," she groaned, "wouldn't you think that I'd remember?"

"You're not any different from the rest of visiting Americans," John said as he spotted a small break in the traffic so that he could urge her beside him as they headed for the other side. "It's even worse when you try to drive over here. Making a turn at an intersection is like planning a tactical maneuver."

"Well, thanks anyhow. If you hadn't grabbed me, I'd probably have been visiting your friend in Harley Street."

After that, the tension between them seemed to disappear as they reached the small Italian restaurant. They selected the house specialty of veal marsala as their main entrée. John ordered some white wine for Paige, but stuck to coffee for himself because of the medication his Harley Street doctor had prescribed.

Actually the veal was a trifle overcooked and the service on the leisurely side, but Paige realized she was having more fun than she could have imagined. John exhibited a side of his nature that she hadn't viewed before; a dry sense of humor that would have captivated any woman. By the time she turned down an offer of spumoni and settled for some expresso, she was hating to see the evening end.

John apparently felt the same way, because it was another half hour before they were back on the sidewalk, waved on their way by the cheerful waiter. The neighborhood streets were almost deserted by that time, and there wasn't a soul to be seen as they leisurely made their way back to the club.

When they reached the intersection where Paige had erred before, she raised a smiling face. "I think I can make it this time," she told John. "There's only that one car, and it's almost a block away."

"Big enough to cross the street alone, eh?" John

said, grinning down at her. "It goes against my Boy Scout instincts, but take off."

"Right. Here I go."

They were so intent on each other, that neither of them noticed a small black car that turned out of the alley halfway down the block and accelerated toward them.

Paige was almost across the street, but John had just stepped off the curb, when she saw the approaching car out of the corner of her eyes and shrieked a warning as it hurtled toward him.

More by instinct than anything else, John half turned and then dived back toward the sidewalk, reaching the curb just as the car careened by.

Paige darted back across the street, completely oblivious to any other oncoming traffic. All she could see was John's crumpled form, lying motionless in the darkness on the sidewalk at her feet.

Chapter Six

"OH, MY GOD!" Paige groaned, as she knelt beside him and pulled his head onto her knees. "John—for heaven's sake—open your eyes!"

His eyelids fluttered and then stayed open. "Why? I'd hate to have that bastard think that he'd missed me in case he comes 'round again." He was struggling to his feet as he spoke, and stooping over to brush the grime from his trousers.

"Are you really all right?" Paige asked nervously. "There's blood on your hand."

"If I could catch up with that blasted driver, he'd have blood more places than his hand. That creep actually seemed to be aiming at me."

"I know." Paige was trying to brush his coat without touching his sore side. "Oh, Lord, I'm sorry," she said as he still winced under her careful ministrations. "There must be a cab around here somewhere."

"Why in the devil do we need a cab?" John frowned down at her. "We're almost at the club now."

"I thought maybe you should go to a doctor," Paige faltered, still upset by the frantic dive he'd taken to avoid being run down.

"That guy in Harley Street would think I was crazy if I showed up twice in one day. Besides, I'm all right. The sidewalk didn't do anything to help my rib, but my pride took the worst beating."

"Unfortunately, you haven't seen your coat and trousers," Paige observed.

John winced again. "I thought I felt a draft in a couple of places. Maybe we'd better go in the back door of the club. That desk clerk might not survive the shock if he takes a look at me."

"It'll do him a world of good." She paused as she stood by the curb again. "Incidentally, I'm not crossing this street if there's a car even in sight."

Fortunately there weren't any more confrontations. At the club, the porter was still snoozing in his chair and the desk clerk was away from his post, so they got in the elevator unobserved.

"I have some Band-Aids in my bag," Paige said when they reached their rooms.

John grimaced and then shrugged. "I guess I'll have to bother you. This scratch on my hand is still oozing. Let me have a shower first, though."

"Can you manage to get your clothes off by yourself?"

Paige didn't even think of the implications of her remark until she saw his sudden amused expression. Then he sobered to nod and say, "I'll give you a shout later, and you can drag out your first-aid kit."

Paige managed an embarrassed nod and ducked into her room without further comment. After washing her hands, she searched through her suitcase for a tube of antiseptic and some adhesive bandages. She kept her thoughts determinedly on the task, trying to ignore what was going on in the room next door. Which was absurd, she kept telling herself. Lord! If she kept on, she'd be worse than Fenella.

She turned on the small television in the corner of her room and listened to a weather report that seemed to cover every part of the world in detail. There was a brief snippet to say clear weather was promised for the London area, but Scotland was in for heavy showers.

That made her think of Lucius, and she decided that a rainstorm served him right. After a trans-Atlantic journey, she rated more than a casual note left with a telephone operator and instructions to take care of excess luggage.

A knock sounded on the connecting door, and she said, "Come in," in a casual, cool tone, that was a triumph. When she saw John in the doorway clad only in a dark blue robe and matching pajama bottoms, she must have shown her surprise.

"Getting out of that damned shirt once was all I could manage tonight." He was tightening the belt of his robe as he spoke.

Paige noticed the pad he'd made out of a hand-kerchief for his hand, and found it was a great way to change the subject. "I've got a box of bandages here," she said, waving him to the small chintz-covered slipper chair, and watched him settle gingerly into it. "Unless you're keen to listen to a discussion on the invasion of garden pests due to a warming trend in the world's weather, I'll turn off the tube," she said, indicating the small set. At his wry expression, she grinned and flipped the switch. "With so few channels, it makes deciding easier," she confided, as she reached for some gauze and the antiseptic. "This is apt to sting," she warned, as she watched him discard the handkerchief.

"I promise not to faint," he drawled, as she dabbed the grazes on the palm of his hand that were still oozing blood. Then, as she put down the antiseptic and turned back with several small elastic bandages, his eyebrows came together. "What the devil—"

"I'm sorry about this," Paige said as she carefully put a bandage with Mickey Mouse emblazoned on it over the worst graze. "My niece gave them to me as a going-away present. She's eight. Would you like Pluto or Donald Duck for the other one?" When he merely grinned, she carefully applied Donald Duck to the smaller laceration. "At least you won't bleed over the sheets now. I'll give you some extra ones for the morning until you can get to a drugstore."

"You mean that you don't make house calls?"

There was something in his voice that made Paige keep her head down and fuss unnecessarily with the top of the antiseptic. "Not as a general rule."

"I did get that feeling," John said slowly. "Considering the shape I'm in right now, maybe it's just as well."

As he started to lever himself out of the chair, Paige put out a restraining hand. "There's no need to dash off. Unless you're in the habit of going to bed at ten-fifteen."

"Hardly." A crooked smile lightened his face for a moment. "Okay. What do you have in mind?"

"There is tea," she said, waving toward the small electrical fixture atop the bureau. "I can't offer anything else, but it could help wash down the pain pills you're supposed to take before you go to bed."

"All right," he sounded resigned. "God! What a great way to celebrate our first night in London!" As she got up to plug in the appliance, he said, "I meant to ask you earlier—what happened to that boss of yours? I thought he'd have plans for your spare time."

Paige suddenly realized that the dinner invitation had driven all thoughts of Lucius's defection from her head. "Actually, he isn't even in the city," she said, watching boiling water pour down onto the cup. After letting the tea bag steep for a short time, she carefully handed over the cup and saucer before making a second one for herself.

John was watching her closely. "What do you mean?"

"Just that." She came back to sit on the edge of the bed. "He left a note for me with the telephone operator here. Apparently if he doesn't get back in time to catch the *Luella Eccles* before it sails, he'll fly home."

"You don't sound brokenhearted."

A mischievous smile crossed her features. "That's because I'm not. He's nice enough as an employer, but inclined to think that working hours go 'round the clock." Looking up, she saw John's eyebrows pull together, and she let out an exasperated sigh. "Not that way. At least, he gave up trying after the first month when I turned down some invitations to see his art collection."

"That's a pretty old line," John admitted.

"I know. So old that it surprised me."

"So now it's just a—"

"—Perfectly normal working relationship. The only reason I dreaded meeting him here was that I usually have to tag along taking notes instead of going the places that I'd like to see."

"But you'd planned to take the freighter back to the States with him?"

"In two separate staterooms." Paige suddenly felt that John's probing was more than just idle conversation. "It wasn't any secret. The *Luella* was going to spend a few days in Rotterdam when I arranged for my ticket, and I was going to take the Hook of Holland ferry across to England. That would have given me about a week in London, which was all I could afford."

"Then the professor isn't—"

When he hesitated over a choice of words, she finished the sentence in a no-nonsense tone. "Paying my way? He certainly isn't. On the other hand, I probably would have let him pick up a dinner check or two. Does that brand me a fallen woman?"

"Whoa!" John held up a protective hand. "Don't take my head off. Just humor me a little longer. Does the professor make a habit of vacationing abroad?"

"As a matter of fact, he does." Paige gave him a puzzled look before getting up to take his empty cup and put it back atop the bureau. "That's not unusual in the academic world."

"I realize that, but let's be more specific. How often does your professor sail with the Eccles Line?"

"Most of the time, I think. That's how Hans got to know him originally. Lucius doesn't like flying, and the good part about academic leave is that you usually have time for surface travel."

"So he recommended the freighter when you decided on a trip abroad this time?"

Paige still couldn't see where his line of questioning was leading, but it was better than the battles they'd staged at the beginning of their acquaintance. She shrugged and replied, "That's right. He suggested the *Luella Eccles* because he knew Hans, and said that I'd have someone to talk to in case I was the only passenger on the trip over."

"But I came along to upset all those plans."

"You were hardly around enough to upset anything," she told him dryly. "Until the night of the storm, you seemed to be doing your level best to pretend that *you* were the only passenger."

He tried to settle more comfortably in the small chair, wincing as he touched a sore spot. "Let's just say that I had other things to think about right then."

Paige could have told him that he really hadn't changed, as he sat there looking a lot better than a man had a right to—even in a tailored robe and pajama trousers. The robe lapels had fallen open as he'd moved and there was a considerable expanse of strong, tanned chest on display. Paige felt that she was spending an inordinate amount of time gazing at it, and hoped to heaven that he hadn't noticed. Trying for something—anything— to divert him she said, "I don't understand your interest in the professor. His trip to Scotland just

proves that he's off on another tangent for the
Bloomsbury Group. Although, I really thought
he'd be dragging me down to Sussex to help with
his research there."

"Hold on a minute. What's all this about the
Bloomsbury Group? You mean Virginia Woolf and
that bunch?"

"It's a good thing the professor isn't around to
hear your description," she said, laughing. "Most
of the time the man eats, drinks, sleeps, and probably dreams about the Bloomsbury Group. He's
writing a book about all of them."

"I shouldn't think that would be on the best-
seller list."

"You might be wrong. There was enough sex
and scandal in their doings at the time that they
were a literary soap opera." She saw him still
frowning and asked, "What's the matter? Is something hurting?"

He gave her an ironic glance. "Don't even ask.
I'll be lucky to get out of this chair if I stay here
much longer."

"Maybe it will be better in the morning," Paige
said with a sympathetic glance.

"I hope so. That's it!" He snapped his fingers,
and then looked amused at her sudden start.
"Sorry, I was trying to remember where I'd seen
something about the Bloomsbury Group recently.
It was in the paper I read while I was in that
doctor's waiting room today. Apparently the
Charleston Farmhouse is being reopened after a
burglary. Weren't Virginia Woolf and her sister
Vanessa Bell connected with that place?"

Paige nodded. "The house is famous for the decorative arts of that period. No wonder the professor went north if he couldn't finish his research there. He must have been terribly disappointed."

"Are you?"

She met John's intent glance with a frown. "Am I what?"

"Disappointed that you can't check out the place with him?"

"Look," she said in an exasperated tone, "I've told you over and over—I couldn't care less about his absence. If I want to go see Charleston Farmhouse, I can hire a car or take a train to Sussex."

"That's probably a good idea." He was painfully levering himself out of the chair as he spoke. "I'll look into it."

She stared up at him in amazement, and then slowly got to her own feet. "I don't understand. Why should you care?"

"I thought I'd go along, if you don't mind some masculine company." He limped on over to the open connecting door, and paused halfway through. "You'd probably like to do some shopping in Knightsbridge tomorrow during the day, but maybe we could go to the theater in the evening. I'll check out the arrangements for traveling down to Sussex the next day if that's okay."

Paige's heartbeat had sped up so much on that invitation that it thundered in her ears, and it was an effort to keep her voice casual. "It sounds fine. Will you make the reservations?"

He nodded, his hand on the doorknob. "We can look over the theater guide at breakfast and decide what we want to see. Anything else?"

Paige was feeling as if she'd already won a prize

in the lottery, so she shook her head. "If there's anything you need in the night—" she broke off as she noticed an amused expression come over his face. "You know what I mean," she faltered.

"Oh, yes. You have a talent with words." There was more than a touch of irony in his voice and expression. "Give me a shout when you're ready to go down to breakfast."

Paige watched him close the door firmly behind him. Evidently he'd read her mind again. She wasn't so sure that she'd managed to read his. However, there was always tomorrow, and tomorrow sounded promising.

Chapter Seven

WHEN PAIGE'S TRAVEL alarm went off the next morning, she was happy to see sunlight edging the drapes she'd drawn on the window overlooking Sloane Street. She yawned and got out of bed slowly, wishing she'd allowed herself another hour. Then she remembered the prospect of shopping in Knightsbridge plus sharing a breakfast table with John, and her lethargy disappeared. On the way to the bathroom, she put an ear to the connecting door to see if there were any activity, but couldn't pick up even the muted sound of television news.

It didn't matter, she told herself, as she turned on the shower. There was plenty of time, and she'd rather go knocking on his door when she was properly dressed.

Barely ten minutes had passed, and she was brushing her teeth, clad only in a damp bath towel when she heard John knocking on the door in question.

She cast an appalled glance in the mirror and then, as there was another series of knocks, she wiped the moisture from her forehead and hurried to open the door a crack.

John looked startled as she peered around the

edge. Naturally he was neatly dressed with only damp hair to testify that his shower hadn't been long before. "Hell, I'm sorry," he said, his glance obviously going over parts of her towel. "I guess I just took it for granted that you'd be ready."

"Can you give me a few minutes more?" she asked, making a grab for the towel as it started to slip.

"Sure thing." He was eyeing her grasp on the towel with evident amusement. "Would you like me to wait here?"

Her lips twitched, but her voice was firm. "I'd like you to go down to the dining room and commandeer a table for us, preferably with some orange juice to go with it. I'll meet you there."

"Pity." For a man who was on the stern side, he seemed to find her dishabille and embarrassment very amusing. "Coffee or tea?"

"Or me?" Paige's response was out before she was aware of it, and she was so horrified that she almost forgot to hang onto the towel.

"That possibility did occur to me," he admitted.

Before he could say any more, she cut in, "Tea, please. I'll switch to coffee later on." She was the one who closed the door between them then, but there was no disguising the masculine chuckle that came through it.

Nothing like presenting a smooth, sophisticated facade, she told herself irritably, as she pulled a comb through her hair a few minutes later. By then, she'd donned a hunter green pullover to go with a brown tweed skirt, while the silk scarf at her throat picked up the colors of both. Her beige gabardine raincoat would have to serve double duty as a topcoat, she decided as she slipped into a pair of brown loafers. With any luck, her outfit would make John forget about that damned towel.

When she arrived at the dining room on the ground floor of the club, he rose promptly from a small table by the door to pull out her chair. "Very nice," he said, giving her an approving glance. "A pity nonetheless. However, the British would probably frown on just a towel for breakfast."

"Especially in this club," Paige agreed with a smile. "Probably the foundations would quiver at the very thought. Speaking of damage, how are you surviving this morning?"

"I recognize a change of subject when I hear one," John said, handing a menu to her. "However, I'll go along with it. I feel much better, thanks."

"And the night wasn't too bad?"

He merely grinned at her and shook his head. "I'm ignoring part of it. I was tempted to knock on your door at three and ask if you wanted a game of double solitaire." He took a swallow of his coffee before adding, "After all, you did offer to help."

Paige kept her eyes on the menu. "You should have given it a try. I'm very good at double solitaire."

"And presumably at many other things." He kept his tone bland. "Here comes the waiter. Are you going for that complete breakfast with fried bread and mushrooms?"

"Heavens no. Just toast, please," she told the waiter, as she reached for the glass of orange juice he placed in front of her along with a pot of tea.

"You'll be sorry," John commented when the man disappeared again toward the kitchen. He indicated a neighboring table that was adorned with two silver toast racks and, presumably, stone-cold toast.

"Oh, Lord, I forgot. What are you having?"

"Bacon and eggs with—toast," he admitted ruefully.

"Then I'll snitch a piece of yours while it's hot if it arrives before mine. With luck, we both might have at least one edible slice. I know better than to expect to have it buttered." She took another sip of juice. "Did you check on the theater schedules?"

"Umm." He reached in the inner pocket of his sport coat and pulled out a brochure of current theater offerings. "Put your attention on this and try not to notice the thin place on the elbow of my coat."

"Let me see," Paige directed, and then shook her head when he displayed the torn fabric. "You can hardly see that it's a little thin. Unless you want to spend the day shopping for a new wardrobe."

"Savile Row comes a long way behind the British Museum on my list today."

"You'll be all right if you don't try any boarding-house reaches," she assured him.

"In that case, would you pass the milk, please? This coffee needs something."

Despite the cold toast and bitter coffee, breakfast was another pleasant interval. They decided that rather than see any of the crop of revivals, they'd opt for a mystery play with a famous actor.

"And if you can't get that—try for anything that sounds like fun," Paige said, handing the brochure back to John. "It's so great being here that it really doesn't matter."

"Right." He tucked the brochure in his coat pocket and pushed his plate away. "What's on your agenda for today?"

"Shopping." Paige's eyes sparkled. "I'm torn between Bond Street and Knightsbridge. With luck, I can get in both before dinner."

"Are you sure you feel like forsaking all that for a day in the country tomorrow if I can arrange transportation to Sussex?"

"It would be nice to get out in the countryside, but—"

"But what?"

"Are you sure that *you* want to spend time looking around that part of the world? The Bloomsbury Group is definitely an acquired taste."

"Have you acquired it?" He was watching her carefully.

"Just a little bit," she said, wondering at his interest. "Since I've done research with the professor, I've been exposed to it constantly. It would be nice to see some of the locales I've read about, but I'll admit that shopping at Harrods is more my usual thing."

"Honest as well as fetching," he said, putting his napkin on the table before pushing back his chair.

"Really fetching," she said somewhat bitterly. "Especially in a storm at sea."

"That green look wasn't your best, but I can wholly recommend this morning's towel scenario. Hello, who's this?"

Paige followed his glance and saw the telephone

operator she'd conferred with the night before heading toward their table. "Oh, damn," she groaned. "Maybe the professor's back in town, after all."

"Relax." John got to his feet as the other woman bustled up.

"Do sit down," the operator was in a discreet black that the club seemed to favor for its minions. "I'm so sorry to disturb your breakfast, Miss Collins, but somehow a message for you didn't get delivered."

Paige's sigh was audible. "That's all right. I suppose it's another call from Professor Smith."

The woman's anxious expression became even more acute. "Why, no. There's nothing more from Professor Smith than the one I told you about. This was a Mr. Deiber. Hans Deiber."

"Hans?" Paige frowned and turned a puzzled look toward John. "He must be in town today."

"Not today. At least, not that I know." The operator sounded as if she'd just like to get her message delivered and leave. A telling glance from the maître d' as he passed the table reinforced her desire. "It was yesterday afternoon, after you checked in," she went on hurriedly. "Evidently you didn't answer your phone or perhaps you were out."

"It doesn't matter," Paige assured her. "What was the message?"

"You were supposed to meet him if possible. A restaurant in Piccadilly. Would you like the phone number?"

"Not now." Paige looked thoughtful, and then as

the woman hovered, added, "Thank you for letting me know."

"I *am* sorry," the operator backed away, as if she'd been in the presence of royalty, retreating hurriedly from the room.

Paige glanced across the table to see a thoughtful look on John's face. "It's too bad there was a mix-up. Hans is bound to be upset."

"Ummm." He reached for his cup and winced slightly. "That isn't what's bothering me."

"Your rib again?"

"Not entirely. I was wondering how Hans managed to desert the ship when he's in charge of the engine-room repair. It's hard to do any supervising long distance."

"I never thought of that. And he must have been in town if he wanted to meet me in Piccadilly."

"I thought you said you were just casual acquaintances."

Her eyebrows went up at his disapproving tone. "I don't know exactly what it takes to get the idea through your head, but I'm not, repeat not, the slightest bit interested in the chief engineer of the *Luella Eccles*."

"Okay. Okay. So maybe I was a little out of line."

"A little?" Her voice rose. "You were all the way out in left field."

"More tea, madam?" It was the waiter materializing at her elbow.

"Thank you, no. I'm already up to here this morning," Paige said, indicating her throat.

"If you'll just bring the bill, I can sign it," John put in quickly, and then shook his head as the waiter hurried off to add up the check. "What do you want for an apology?" John made no attempt to hide his amusement. "I'd better tell you that I never grovel at breakfast."

"And I'd better tell you that my manners are better after ten o'clock in the morning," Paige told him ruefully. "I think it's a draw."

"Right. So we'll take it that it's not unrequited love that brings Hans to town. It must have been something pretty urgent though, considering the shape of things on the ship." John accepted the check from the waiter and signed it after adding a tip. "Thank you very much."

"Thank you, sir."

"Does everybody in this club do that?" Paige asked, watching the man go back toward the kitchen.

"Do what?"

"He practically pulled on his forelock when he left. My God, this club is like something out of Dickens." She turned to see John frowning again. "Now what's the matter?"

"If it wasn't you that Hans came up to see," he replied slowly, as if thinking aloud, "how about your professor? You said they were old friends."

"Yes, but Lucius isn't here."

"I know that," John said irritably. "But maybe Hans didn't. Especially if the professor's trip up north materialized in a hurry."

She shook her head slowly. "It sounds a little thin to me. I really think you're making too much of this. The man had a chance to get out of Felixstowe for a few hours, and came up to the bright lights. Now, what are you laughing about?"

"The bright lights," John said dryly, gesturing around them. "The paneling in this room must have been put up right after they finished Hampton Court Palace. They're probably still cooking over a fireplace down in the basement here."

"Wrong. They only use the fireplace for toasting forks and crumpets. Never mind—there's a New York-style deli on Sloane Square if you get desperate." She pushed back her chair and stood up. "I'd better get started on my shopping expedition. Will you be okay?"

He was following her out of the room, and pulled up at the carpeted stairs, which led to the main hall of the club. "I'll struggle along and no, I don't need any help crossing streets. Thanks just the same. Do you want to meet down in Piccadilly for an early dinner?"

"That sounds good." Paige was proud of her casual acceptance.

"Okay. How about five o'clock at the garden restaurant of Fortnum's? We can have a drink there, and I promise there isn't any paneling in the place." He started down the corridor beside her toward the elevator. "One more thing."

She looked up at him inquiringly.

"If there are any more calls from Hans or your professor friend, don't agree to meet them. Tell them you're booked for the time you're here. Okay?"

If he'd sounded the least bit like an eager swain or the slightest bit jealous of any other masculine attention, Paige would have been over the rainbow with joy. Instead his tone was authoritative, and there was an expression on his face that boded ill for anyone who disagreed with him. It was the same look that he'd had most of the way across the Atlantic when he'd encountered her, and Paige reacted predictably. "Some people say, 'I'd rather you didn't' or 'would you please.' Instead you're giving orders again." She stopped in front of the elevator and punched the button with unnecessary force. "It's not that I mind, but it probably wouldn't hurt for us to have a drink with Hans tonight if he's still in town."

"I doubt very much if he'd be in favor of that suggestion," he said dryly.

"I don't see why." Paige automatically moved aside when the elevator arrived and the porter tottered out with two big suitcases. She put her hand on the edge of the door to hold it.

"Just take my word for it," John said.

"Aren't you going up to your room?" she asked when he turned toward the front door instead of following her into the elevator.

"Not now. I'll see you at Fortnum's, if not before."

She watched him leave before she went in and punched the elevator button for her floor. If it hadn't been undignified, she would have been clutching the back of his sport coat to find out just what he meant by his last remarks.

They were still on her mind when she went into Fortnum and Mason's crowded restaurant in late afternoon. By then, Paige felt as if she'd taken part in a six-hour marathon. During the last hour, she'd hobbled back to the club to change into the one-occasion dress she'd brought with her—a deep purple velvet with a scalloped neckline and flared skirt. The stole she'd wrapped around her shoulders was of the same material, and lined in cashmere for warmth. Even so, she was happy to get into the comfortable steam-heated restaurant. At first she didn't recognize the tall man in an elegant charcoal suit who was getting to his feet at a table nearby. Then she took a second look, shook her head in disbelief, and walked over to sit down beside him.

"I refuse to believe that suit was in your suitcase all the time at the club," she said to John. "You did visit Savile Row, after all."

He shook his head and, if Paige hadn't known better, seemed slightly embarrassed by her frankly admiring glance. "Definitely not Savile Row, but just an obliging tailor. The same one who promised to mend the holes in my sport coat and get it back to the club by tomorrow morning." He let his own glance wander over her. "That's quite a transformation for you. It's a good thing you didn't appear in that at dinner on the freighter or the navigator would never have found the English Channel."

He'd leaned over to help her slip the stole from her shoulders, and it seemed to Paige that he was reluctant to take his hands away. So that he wouldn't notice how even his touch affected her, she said lightly, "I'll be fine just so long as we don't have to walk to the theater. This stole is great for effect, but not much for warmth. Do you suppose I could have a cup of tea instead of something with ice?"

"I don't see why not. I'll keep you company with coffee. We'll order dinner after we warm up a bit," he told the hovering waitress.

Paige was looking around the crowded restaurant. "Almost every table is full, and it's early."

"If you listen to the conversations, you'll find they're mostly Americans who've made this sort of a 'home away from home.' You can recognize most of the items on the menu, and the service allows you to get to the theater on time."

"And will we?" When he surveyed her quizzically, she went on. "Have a theater to go to? If you know what I mean."

He pretended to shudder. "Grammar is an endangered species with you. But yes, we have tickets for that mystery thriller, thanks to a cancellation. I hope you'll like it."

"Anything behind footlights is great!" She pushed her purse aside so that two teapots and a cup and saucer could be put in front of her. By the time a pitcher of milk was added, there wasn't much room left on the table.

"What are you laughing about?" John asked, when the waitress had bustled off again.

"This array of silver plate. You just have a cup of coffee. I feel as if I should be serving tea to a regiment. It's much more impressive than a cup of hot water with a tea bag on a saucer."

"Well, cherish it. Once you're back aboard the ship, a tea bag will be the order of the day. Speaking of the ship, did you have any more messages from Hans or your professor?" Catching her warning glance, he changed his question, "I mean, *the* professor."

"Nothing," she said after taking a sip of her steaming tea. "Now you can bring me up to date.

Why did you say this morning that you didn't think Hans would want to meet us?"

"Well, there's the obvious. If a man has plans for a cozy twosome, he's not going to be thrilled about sharing a threesome."

She surveyed him thoughtfully over the rim of her cup. "But that's not the only reason is it?"

He gave her a considering look, as if debating his options. "No, not really," he said finally. When she made no attempt to alter the silence that lengthened between them, he said, "Probably it's because we work for the same company."

Her eyes widened at this newest revelation. "Wait a minute—you mean you work for the Eccles Line, too?"

John nodded.

When he didn't say anything, she kept on probing. "Hans must know it. Do the rest of the officers?"

For the first time, a glimmer of amusement showed on his face. "Oh, yes. It isn't exactly a secret."

"Only from the passenger section." She put her teacup down on the saucer so decisively that some of it spilled over the edge, and she grimaced. "Damn!"

"Serves you right." He watched her extract a paper handkerchief from her purse and mop up. "I'm glad you didn't use that cloth napkin—the waitress has us under her eagle eye."

"It would be nice if she'd help instead of just manning an observation post," Paige said irritably, and then looked abashed when a busboy came hurrying up with a clean saucer. "Why do I keep getting in hot water?" she asked after he'd gone.

"Hot tea in this case," John corrected with a chuckle. "It's probably because of those red streaks in your hair."

"And might have something to do with the man who's been letting me make an almighty fool of myself. No wonder you knew what was going to happen to the ship the night of the storm." She fixed him with an accusing glare. "The captain told me that this crew has three voyages on and then three off. Are you going to work on the next three?"

He shook his head. "I do have my papers, but I haven't been going to sea lately. To work, I mean."

"Then this is a busman's holiday for you?"

"You could say that."

"I'm glad I did, because it's obvious that you're not going to," she replied, making no attempt to hide her exasperation. "If you were paid by the word for your conversational gems, you'd go broke in a hurry. Let me guess—can we rule out a mad desire to get reacquainted with Fenella as the reason for this trip?"

"Lord, yes." He was gesturing for the waitress to bring some menus. "I'm hungry—shall we go ahead and order dinner?"

She nodded reluctantly. "Whatever you say. But don't think that I'm ignoring the fat red herring that you're serving up for the first course."

He gave a tut-tut at the accusation. "You're letting your imagination run away from you again. How do lamb chops sound? We have plenty of time for the grill. The grill in the kitchen, that is," he added with a slow grin.

She smiled back reluctantly. "Lamb chops will be fine. I hope their chef has better luck than I'm having. Incidentally, you don't have to apologize for wanting to avoid the freighter officers while you're here. I've been keeping my fingers crossed all day that the professor doesn't get tired of Scotland and come back to London again."

"Maybe the best safeguard is for us to take our phones off the hook tonight. By the way, I've arranged for a car and driver out of Lewes tomorrow."

She stared at him, completely amazed. "Then you're serious about wanting to check out that old neighborhood of the Bloomsbury Group?"

"As of today, I'm a self-proclaimed expert on the place," he said pulling a pamphlet from his inside coat pocket. "I thought we might enjoy a drive around, and drop in at a few of their old haunts like Charleston Farmhouse. Do you approve of the plan?"

"It sounds great," she said, nervously fiddling with one of the forks that had been put in front of her. "I'm just surprised, that's all. Bloomsbury aficionados are usually gray-haired, and don't often stray from college campuses."

"Maybe it was Virginia and Vanessa's sexy lifestyle that attracted me." He grinned as Paige considered it before shaking her head. "Something tells me I'm in a 'no win' situation," John said, and then added deliberately, "What happened on your shopping expedition today?"

Paige decided that it was best to let him change

the subject. As far as tomorrow's excursion went, she would have been happy to follow him barefoot through the unheated basement of the British Museum. In contrast, a carefree day driving around the Sussex countryside was manna from heaven. And before that, there was the prospect of a good dinner and a marvelous evening at the theater. Only an idiot would be fool enough to say anything to upset the plans.

As it turned out, their dinner was delicious and the play was fun, as well. They were even fortunate in finding a cab to take them back to the club afterward, so that Paige didn't have to pretend that her thin stole was really warm enough.

The lobby of the club was deserted, except for a sleepy night clerk who barely looked up from his newspaper long enough to hand them their room keys.

They were still discussing how much time they'd need to allow for breakfast before heading to the railroad station when Paige was unlocking the door to her room. Since she was glancing over her shoulder at John, the first evidence she had that anything was wrong was his sudden frown. "What's the matter?" she asked.

He put his hands on her shoulders and turned her to face the room. "I presume you didn't leave it like that," he said in an ominous tone.

Paige stared in disbelief at the chaos in front of her; her belongings had been taken from the suitcase and strewn ruthlessly around. Even the beds hadn't been spared, the linen was stripped from them, and the mattresses were pulled partway off the springs. Paige leaned back into John's solid frame for comfort. "Good God!" she muttered, "it never occurred to me that in a place like this—"

John gave her a reassuring hug before urging her forward. "You'd better check and see what's missing."

She nodded and let him close the door behind them. Looking at her scattered belongings, she said bitterly, "This must have been a great disappointment to them—there really weren't any valuables for them to steal. I left my traveler's checks and passport down in the office safe."

"What about jewelry?"

She fingered the single strand of pearls at her throat. "This is all I brought with me. Do you suppose I can straighten things up, or do I have to leave everything as it is and report it to the office?"

"That desk clerk looked like the only security officer around at this hour, so I think we might as well put the place in order. Unless you'd like to spend the rest of the night in my room and display the evidence tomorrow morning."

She considered the possibilities for a moment and then shook her head. "It isn't worth all the trouble. By the time we call in the powers that be, we'd have to cancel our trip to Sussex."

"You're right about that. Well, we can at least leave the door open between our rooms for the rest of the night so you won't have to worry about any more intruders."

She watched him push the mattresses back in place as she asked ruefully, "Am I wrong or have we been plagued by minor catastrophes for the last day or so?"

He was pulling the spread on the nearest bed back into place as he looked across at her and nodded. "I wasn't going to mention it, but I think somebody is trying to discourage us in every way possible. Tomorrow it will be a good idea to be very careful crossing streets and keep all your valuables in the safe."

She put her suitcase back on the luggage rack, and tried not to acknowledge the fear that coursed through her. "Then you don't think it's over?"

He took a deep breath and shook his head. "No, damn it. I'm afraid that it's just begun."

Chapter Eight

DESPITE THEIR FOREBODINGS, the next twelve hours passed as uneventfully as a travel agent's dream. When Paige finally got to sleep with the connecting door open, the rest of the night went by quickly. Both of them were surprised that they overslept, which meant a hurried cup of coffee and roll at the railroad station before boarding a train to Lewes, where John had arranged for the car and driver to meet them.

Paige was wearing beige wool slacks and a pale yellow crew-neck sweater for the day, and John had donned his mended sport coat and slacks. The London tailor had done his work well, and it would have taken a very close look to see any damage.

Having first-class tickets gained them a compartment all to themselves on the train, but when Paige commented on it, John said calmly that they were merely going against the commuter stream. After bringing her another cup of coffee from the buffet car as soon as they left London, he'd pointedly buried himself in a brochure on the Bloomsbury Group in Sussex, leaving Paige to admire the suburban towns and read the London paper he'd bought at a station newsstand.

The ride to Lewes was just long enough to be interesting, and not so long that she was tempted to wander up and down the train to see what their fellow passengers were like. The silence in their compartment was comfortable, and she knew enough about John by then to realize he was paying her a compliment of sorts. If he'd felt the necessity of making conversation on the journey, she had a sneaking suspicion that he would have come alone and left her to find her way around London for the day.

When the train ground to a halt at the Lewes station, he put the brochure in his pocket, checked his watch, and nodded with satisfaction. "Right on time," he said, getting to his feet so that he could open their compartment door into the side corridor.

"Do you want this newspaper?" Paige asked, lingering by her seat.

He shook his head. "That was just to keep you amused in case you didn't have a book."

She put her head to one side and gave him a provocative glance. "Actually I did, but it didn't seem polite to pull it out of my purse."

"Now you know better," he said over his shoulder, as he led the way to the end of the car and the door opening onto the station's concrete walkway. "Let's hope that our car's out in front."

Paige stayed by his side as they went up the stairway from the tracks, and then made their way through the almost deserted station. As soon as they went outside, she saw the small gray car with an elderly man leaning against the front fender. He straightened as they approached and asked politely, "Mr. Winthrop?"

"Right," John said, nodding in response. "This is Miss Collins who'll be going with us."

"Very good, sir. My name's Lawrence. You should both be comfortable in the backseat, or would one of you prefer to sit in front with me?"

"We can manage in back, thanks," John said. After they'd gotten in, he waited for Lawrence to slide behind the wheel before saying, "I thought we might take a look at the Berwick Church and then," he glanced at his watch again, "maybe take a short break for lunch before we go on to Charleston Farmhouse. Do you know of a place to eat on the road?"

"There's a good pub that's not far out of the way if that kind of meal appeals to you," Lawrence said, checking with them in the rearview mirror. "Otherwise we can come back to town here for a more elaborate menu."

John looked at Paige inquiringly. "The pub, by all means," she said without hesitation. "I haven't had a chance to try one since we've been here."

"Good enough." That slight smile lightened John's expression again. "And how about the rest of the itinerary. Okay with you?"

"I probably shouldn't admit this—but it's great to have somebody else making decisions," she told him. "I think you must have had some influence on the temperature, too. Or have you been enjoying this balmy fall weather all week?" she asked Lawrence, as he started the engine and prepared to pull out into the traffic in front of the small station.

"It's been very nice, miss," he assured her. "That should make your drive much more pleasant. Especially if you want to walk around the garden at Charleston Farmhouse."

John's eyebrows went up slightly, and he turned to Paige, saying in a low voice, "The Bloomsbury reputation must be wider than I thought."

She smiled. "There are lots of curious souls who want to see their homes—especially Monk's House, where Virginia Woolf left a note for her husband in 1941 and then walked down to the river to drown herself. It was the kind of thing that tabloids are made of."

"If there's time, we'll stop by there on the way back to the station," John said.

From the tone of his voice, it was clear that he wasn't taking it very seriously, and Paige felt a touch of relief. Especially after spending so many of her working hours with a man to whom the members of the Bloomsbury group were almost sacrosanct.

By then, the driver had cleared the outskirts of Lewes and was heading out through the green, gently rolling Sussex countryside. There were small farm holdings on either side of the road, but the general atmosphere was peace and quiet—a far cry from the bustle of London earlier.

It was a welcome change, and Paige relaxed beside John, curious to see what the day's schedule would bring. Even their short detour to the Berwick churchyard for a look at the gravestones of Duncan Grant and Vanessa Bell seemed fit and proper. The old church itself was deserted, and the air inside seemed cold and untouched—like the quiet cemetery just beyond its steps. Paige walked quickly out in the fall sunshine again, happy for the warmth on her back.

"If it's not too early for your lunch, the pub I had in mind is close by," Lawrence told them before starting the car again.

"Is it a cheerful place?" Somehow that seemed more important to Paige just then than the quality of food.

"Very nice, miss. They have tables outside, too, although the wind's a bit brisk for that today."

"All right?" John was frowning slightly as he saw her expression.

"Fine, thanks." She put aside her sudden feeling of depression and managed a smile. "I should have warned you that I'm not very good with cemeteries. And that one," she gestured behind her as Lawrence pulled out into the quiet narrow road, "seemed especially sad. I guess I expected to find it more manicured, and not just a neglected place where the grass needed reseeding. Even the church seemed dead."

"Your imagination is running riot again. Remember, this is the English countryside, and history is never dead. Or at least that's what's implied in my trusty brochure."

"I promise to do better," she said, sorry that she'd let her reactions show so vividly. "From what I've read, Charleston Farmhouse is full of cheerful color."

Lawrence must have been listening because he cut in. "Indeed, it is, miss. You're very fortunate to arrive today. The authorities closed it last week after a theft, but now everything's back to normal."

"Well, that's good. It would be a shame to come

this far and not get a chance to go through the place." She turned to John, who seemed to be concentrating on the scenery. "Don't you agree?"

It was obvious he wasn't really interested in the conversation, because it was a moment or two before he nodded. Then changing the subject, he said to Lawrence, "I hope this pub you're talking about has something good on the menu. Brit Rail stations aren't known for their breakfasts."

"You'll like it, I'm sure," the driver said confidently over his shoulder.

It was about fifteen minutes later before he turned up a winding lane, and came to a stop in front of a stone building that looked as if it had once been a one-room cottage, but had been enlarged in helter-skelter fashion. There were already a half-dozen cars parked along the edge of the narrow lane, and two of the iron tables on the patio were occupied with diners. "You go right on in," Lawrence told John and Paige as he came around to let them out. "A friend of mine works in the kitchen, so I'll be in there chatting with him. Just send word when you're ready to leave."

"How far is it to Charleston Farmhouse from here?" John asked, looking at his watch again.

"Only about twenty minutes. You'll make it before closing time very nicely," the driver assured him.

"Right, we'll see you later," John said, taking Paige's elbow to steer her down the gravel path.

The crude wooden tables and chairs that constituted the furnishings of the small pub were a little disconcerting, but Paige forgot the decor and damp air when a cheerful waitress came from behind the bar with handwritten menus.

After a short discussion, Paige and John settled for a Sussex version of a Monte Cristo sandwich, and ordered small lagers while they waited for their food.

Paige wrinkled her nose slightly at the first sip of the warm beer. "I'd make a terrible drunk," she confessed. "Especially when the stuff is lukewarm. The only time it really tastes good is when the temperature is over a hundred, and even the glass has to be frosty."

"We can solve that," John said, getting to his feet. "What do you want to change it for? Lemonade? Bitter lemon? I doubt if they have American ginger ale."

"It doesn't matter. Any of the above," Paige said gratefully, pushing the lager aside and helping herself to the package of crisps that had been put down between them.

He was back in no time with a bottle of bitter lemon and a clean glass. "I got word from the kitchen that our sandwiches are practically on the way."

"Good. In the meantime, put these out of my reach," Paige said, shoving the crisps toward him. "I have no willpower."

He grinned at that. "How strange. From what I've seen, you're a woman chock-full of willpower."

"And from what I've seen—you're loaded with the stuff yourself."

"Not always." He focused his attention on his glass and absently rubbed his thumb down the side of it. "You've caught me a little out of my league."

"I don't understand—"

"I'm not surprised, and I'm not in a position to explain just yet." His glance came up to meet hers then. "Give me a little more time, will you?"

"Does it have anything to do with the reason you didn't report the break-in at the club last night?"

He nodded and sat back in his wooden chair. "After you said that nothing was missing, I couldn't believe that it was just some sneak thief who'd broken in."

"You think someone chose my room deliberately? But why? What could he have been looking for?"

"God only knows. I sure as hell don't—"

He broke off as the waitress brought their plates of hot sandwiches over to the table. Cutlery was pulled from a deep pocket in her apron and placed without ceremony in front of them. She surveyed the table with satisfaction. "Righto. That should do it. Let me know if you'd like a refill of your drinks."

"Perhaps some coffee," Paige said tentatively.

The woman nodded, but said, "I'll bring it when you've finished your sandwiches," and headed back to the bar.

"You should know better by now," John said, chuckling as he used his knife and fork to cut into the steaming sandwich. "Tea comes at four in the afternoon, and coffee comes *after* the meal except at breakfast. It's no use trying to buck the system."

"You're right. I've lost too many times. Anyhow, the bitter lemon will serve." She started to laugh as she surveyed the rough wooden table.

He stopped with his fork halfway to his mouth, "Now what?"

"I was just thinking that after dinner last night, we're down to the bare essentials today. No place mats—no condiments—"

"I can do without that," he said, moving uncomfortably on his chair, "but I'd pay extra for some padding on the furniture."

"I'm a little surprised that this is on your list of 'things to see,' " Paige said to John after lunch, as they were being driven down the two-lane road toward Charleston Farmhouse. "The professor didn't rate it very high in his Bloomsbury Group studies. He said that it was just a summer boardinghouse before Vanessa Bell moved in with Duncan Grant."

"I don't expect a stately home," John said calmly. "My brochure says that it has a unique style. Apparently the paintings are colorful, even if they're not in the 'old master' category." He saw a frown crease her forehead, "Now what have I said?"

She made a helpless gesture with open palms. "I've just missed all the way around. When it comes to art, I would have sworn you were a Turner or Gainsborough man rather than some of the bizarre stuff by Duncan Grant."

"Which shows you should never prejudge the male sex," John told her solemnly. "Remind me to make you a list of my other vices on the train ride back."

"If you do, that will be the only information you've furnished since we docked at Felixstowe," Paige said. When he didn't respond, she made a point of staring out the window on her side of the car, until a little later when Lawrence slowed and drove carefully up a rutted driveway toward a nondescript farmhouse atop a small hill.

"Charleston," he said proudly. "And you've just enough time to tour the place before they close." Gesturing with one hand, he added, "The gift shop's over there to the left if you want any souvenirs. The garden at the side of the house is the one that your American lady restored so nicely. Of course, at this time of year it's not much of a showplace, but in the spring it's a fair treat." He drew up and parked in a gravel area that already had several cars in it. "I'll wait for you here, but you'll have to move sharp, or you'll run out of time before you've finished the house tour."

Under his eagle eye, Paige was reluctant to admit that she didn't really want an entire house tour, although she obediently got out of the car and waited for John to come around and join her.

"You go ahead," he told her as he closed his door. "I'll just take a look in the gift shop and then meet you in the farmhouse. Okay?"

Paige didn't have a chance to object, since he was already striding toward the small gift shop that Lawrence had pointed out earlier. Another facet of his character that she'd misread, she thought as she shrugged and turned toward the front entrance of the old farmhouse. If anyone had told her that John was the type to linger in a gift shop, she would have said they were crazy. She shook her head again and walked on.

When the woman guarding the door asked for her admission ticket, Paige looked blankly back at her and then reached for her purse. "I'm sorry," she began, "I didn't realize."

"You're American, aren't you?" The gray-haired lady consulted a paper on the hall table beside her. "Miss Collins? Come in. It's all been arranged." She frowned then and looked over Paige's shoulder. "But where is Mr. Winthrop?"

"In the gift shop at the moment, but he'll be along shortly."

"I do hope so," the woman told her. "You're cutting it a bit fine. Elsie here," she gestured toward another woman who was hovering nearby, "will be pleased to take you around. You'll start in the dining room over there to the left. One of the most charming and cheerful areas, I think."

After that, Paige didn't have time to make any comments or wonder what had happened to John, because the guide took her work seriously and didn't miss a feature of the decorations, the furniture—even bizarre as some of it was—and the pictures on the wall. John joined them, finally, as they started up to the second floor and melted the guide's annoyance with a smile that left her blushing. But from then on, the woman acted like a horse headed for the stable. Her facts and figures were rattled off with machine-gun precision, and fifteen minutes later John and Paige were ushered from the workroom at the rear of the house with an admonition to "be sure and enjoy the garden before you leave."

By then, the afternoon sun had disappeared under a cloud cover that made the garden less appealing than earlier. Paige and John took the obligatory walk around the paths under the eye of another guide—this time a man who looked as if he doubled as a gardener.

When they finally arrived back at the car, John glanced down at her weary face and asked, "Want to bother with the gift shop or just head back to the railway station?"

"I'm not keen on gift shops. Besides, the professor probably has all the books on this place already. But didn't you want to visit the Monk's House at Rodmell?"

"I can give it a miss. Right now, I think we'd better catch an earlier train back to London. In the rush to leave this morning, I forgot to call the Eccles office in Felixstowe. They might have changed the ship's sailing time and been trying to get in touch with us."

"Heavens, I'd forgotten all about that," Paige confessed, as John opened the car door for her before he went to tell Lawrence of their change of plans.

It wasn't until she and John were on the train back that she commented on her reaction to Charleston. "I guess I expected more, since I'd read so much about it. The decor was certainly extravagant, but when you paint over wooden cupboards and doors, they have a tendency just to look like old painted cupboards and doors. I think even Gainsborough would have had trouble in those surroundings." She eyed the wrapped package that he had by his side. "Did you find something you liked at the gift shop?"

"Sort of." John hesitated a minute, and then pulled a slim art folio from the wrappings. "It shows some of Duncan Grant's best works from the cottage. Take a look."

Paige took it from him and rifled through the pages, pausing occasionally to read the captions below the pictures. "It's more interesting having seen the place," she said finally as she handed it back to him.

"That sounds like faint praise," he said wryly, tucking the book away in its wrapping once again.

"I'm sorry, but Duncan Grant's works aren't my cup of tea, no matter what the critics say." She rested her head back against the top of her seat in their compartment. "Actually, I had a great day. It was nice to get away from London and down to the quiet of the country. And now, when the professor starts to drone on about the Bloomsbury Group, I can try to make an intelligent response." She looked up to see John staring at her with a bemused expression. "Do I have a smudge on my nose or something? It wouldn't be surprising," she added, gesturing around the train compartment. "There's almost as much dust in here as in my living room at home. I got spoiled on the ship with Salvatore taking care of the cabin. There wasn't a speck of dirt to be found anywhere." Then, as another thought occurred, "You don't think we're going to be late for the sailing, do you?"

"Not really. We can call as soon as we get back to the club, and then maybe have a posh dinner somewhere, since we're a little late to get theater tickets."

"That sounds wonderful, if you think your cracked

rib can take it. You've been awfully stoic about the whole thing."

"Probably because it's not all that bad. The only thing that's suffering now is my stomach. That pub lunch was fine as far as it went, but—"

"—It went a long time ago," she agreed, smiling at his rueful look. "There's always a cup of tea from the buffet."

"Hardly worth it now," he said, reading the name of the station they were just then pulling into. "We should be back in the city in another twenty minutes. Is that all right with you?"

She nodded, feeling suddenly shy at discovering this more kindly side to the man sitting across from her. He'd been attractive even when he'd been at his most aloof—now when he was being the considerate escort in every way, the man was devastating.

Somewhere along the line, she'd fallen head over heels in love with John Winthrop, and that most definitely wasn't on her schedule. She took a deep breath and let it out slowly, desperately determined to keep the revelation to herself.

Chapter Nine

IT WAS FORTUNATE that for their remaining time in London, Paige didn't have time to dwell on her emotional state. When they arrived back at the club, there was a message waiting for them to phone the head office of the Eccles Line immediately.

John waited only until they were up in his room before putting through the call, and had an uneasy look on his face when he finally hung up the receiver.

"What's happened?" Paige asked, trying to ignore the tension in the air.

"They've advanced the sailing time. We'll have to be aboard by four tomorrow afternoon. That means we should leave here right after midday to play it safe. I'd better check on the express trains that connect."

"Well, at least that gives us tonight and the morning for any last-minute shopping and stuff," she said, keeping her voice light despite her disappointment.

He stood up and strode over to the window, looking down at busy Sloane Street. "That's the devil of it. I'm afraid dinner tonight is out, too.

There's a man I have to see since the plans have changed."

It was an effort for her to smile and walk over to the door between their rooms. "You'll probably want to get along then."

"Paige—wait." His command caught her on the threshold, and she looked back at him, trying not to reveal her feelings. "I'm sorry," he said softly, showing that her attempt hadn't been very successful. "Maybe we can take a raincheck."

"Somewhere. Sometime." She kept her voice level. "It's a date. Now I think I'll go in and wash some of the Sussex topsoil away. Are we meeting for breakfast?"

His relief at her acceptance was obvious, which didn't help either. Neither did his hearty, "You bet. I can't wait to have my last cup of coffee downstairs. Knock on my door in the morning when you're ready."

"Right." Paige shut the connecting door behind her, and a few minutes later heard his hall door close. Obviously he hadn't wasted any time going to his scheduled meeting. For an instant, she wondered if it had been an excuse to meet another Fenella-type who lived in London. Then she shook her head in disgust at her lack of faith. She'd barely realized she'd fallen in love with the man, and already she was accusing him of having a nice little crumpet on the side.

An evening with BBC television after a lonely dinner didn't help her mood. It was with relief she turned off a program on Albanian economic problems, when it was finally time to get in bed. Although she had tried to subdue stray thoughts of John, she was sure that he hadn't returned by midnight, which didn't improve her mood either.

When her alarm sounded in the morning, she groaned and got out of bed slowly. It was one thing to wake up with a headache after a splendid night on the town, and quite another to feel rotten after a "boil it, eat it, forget it" dinner and an evening noted only for changing channels on television.

It was on her way to the shower that she saw a small slip of paper shoved under the connecting door, and her spirits sank even lower. She leaned against the wall as she opened the note, and found two brief sentences in John's writing. "Sorry about missing breakfast," he wrote. "Meet you here at noon, and we'll have to check out right afterward." There was a capital *J* at the bottom, but that was all. Hardly the kind of thing to wrap up in violet ribbon and store away. Which proved that she was right to keep her emotions well hidden, she told herself, and tried to feel good about it as she stepped into the shower.

She decided she couldn't take another meal in the formal dining room of the club and instead stopped by Sloane Square for coffee and a piece of toast. After that, there was an hour or two to pick up the small gifts she planned to carry back home with her and arrange for some special china for her parents to be shipped.

As always, everything took longer than she'd thought, and finally she saw that she only had forty-five minutes before the noon deadline that John had mentioned.

Once back at the club, packing her slim belongings didn't take long. Rather than delaying their departure, Paige decided to take her bag down to the desk and check out. When she finally corralled the attention of the cashier and asked for her bill, the woman looked surprised.

"Why, that's already been taken care of, Miss Collins," she said, after looking through a worn ledger.

"You must be mistaken. There isn't anyone who'd pay my bill. Unless—" she chewed on her lip uncertainly as she thought about the professor. Perhaps he'd made the gesture because of leaving town so precipitously. "Could I ask who paid it?"

"I suppose so." Consulting the ledger again, the cashier said triumphantly, "Yes, I have it right here. Your account was paid by the Eccles Line. They're paying for Mr. Winthrop's room, too." She closed the thin book with a snap. "I hope you enjoyed your stay with us, Miss Collins."

It was a nice change from "have a good day," but Paige wasn't in the mood to appreciate the difference. She managed to smile, and went back to the front hall of the club where the porter was waiting with her bag.

When she started for the elevator, he spoke up hastily, "Mr. Winthrop came in just a few minutes ago, Miss Collins. I told him you were with the cashier, and he said you might as well wait for him here as he'll be right down. His bag is already here," he added, gesturing toward the door. "Shall I go and hail a cab for you?"

"I guess so," Paige said, feeling as if things were moving a little too fast. "Especially if it's difficult to get one."

The porter nodded, pulling a whistle from his uniform pocket as he went out and turned up Sloane Street where the traffic was thick at midday.

He'd scarcely left, when the elevator door opened and John stepped out, carrying his raincoat over his arm. If he was surprised to see her obediently waiting, he didn't show it. Probably because he was accustomed to giving orders and having them obeyed, Paige thought with resignation.

"Good morning or is it afternoon?" she said, trying a cool approach. "Have you enjoyed your morning?"

"Not particularly," he countered in a tone as unrevealing as hers. "I take it you found my note."

Paige was tempted to reply that she'd had it sealed in plastic for posterity, but another glance at John's stern features made her opt for common sense. "Yes, thanks. I did a little last-minute shopping."

He gave her small shopping bag an intent look. "You must be trying to solve our country's balance of payments by yourself."

"Not really. It has more to do with balancing my checking account. I'm not as pure as I look though—I had a set of china sent to my folks. There *is* something I wanted to ask you before we leave. Did the Eccles Line take care of your bill here, too?"

"Uh-huh." He was moving toward the club entrance as he replied, "It's a courtesy of the passenger department when the ship's schedule is changed for repairs."

"S'funny," she said, trailing behind him. "I've

never heard of that practice before. Do they mention it in their brochures?"

"Hardly," he said in a wry tone. "The Line isn't keen on admitting they have mechanical troubles either to their passengers or freight customers. Is this all you have?" He was looking at her overnight case as he spoke.

"That's it. Except for this," she waved the plastic carrier bag on one finger. "Here comes the porter—I guess he's found a cab for us. At this rate, we shouldn't have any trouble making our connection."

"I guess not."

There was enough weariness in John's tone to make Paige stare at him in surprise. Before she could ask what was wrong, he was through the club doors, helping to load their bags into the taxi at the curb. Paige trailed along after him, wondering if he was going to be in that unhappy frame of mind all the way to the coast. If so, it was a good thing she'd left her paperback where it was easily reachable.

"Just a minute, miss."

The porter's urgent command stopped her with one foot in the cab. She stepped back on the sidewalk with a sudden frown when he came hurrying up, carrying a smart-looking attaché case. "You forgot this," he said reproachfully.

"No, I didn't," she told him. "It doesn't belong to me."

He shoved it into the taxi with the rest of their things. "Maybe not, but the front office said you were supposed to take it with you. We've had it in storage while you've been here."

A light suddenly dawned in Paige's mind. "Oh, Lord. The professor," she said. "I'd forgotten all about it." Then, seeing the impatience on the taxi driver's face, she added hastily to John, "It's all right. I'll explain on the way to the station."

His glance was intent, but he merely nodded. "Okay, get in. I'll take care of things here."

He finished tipping the porter by the time Paige had slid onto the seat, and he got in beside her, letting the elderly man slam the cab door.

"From the smile on his face, you must have gotten the exchange wrong on your tip," Paige said.

"At this moment, it's worth it," John said. He leaned forward to tell the driver, "Liverpool Street station," and watched him close the glass between them before he sat back on the seat and turned to Paige. "Now, tell me about this extra bag. *All* about it," he emphasized.

"You know almost as much as I do," Paige confessed. "When I registered at the club, they said the professor had taken off for the north somewhere. I told you about it before."

"You mentioned *that*. You didn't say anything about left luggage though."

"To be honest, it slipped my mind until the porter came out with it just now. I guess I was so surprised that the professor had deserted me, that his darned baggage didn't register. He's probably decided to fly home, and didn't want to pay any excess luggage charge. I'm surprised he didn't leave more than one, but maybe his conscience started to bother him." She became aware that John's forbidding expression had changed again, and he was looking at her quizzically—even with some amusement. "I wish you'd make up your mind," she told him impulsively. "Earlier I was getting the cold and stony—like something that had been left too long on the slab at the local fish market. And now, you—"

"—Look as if I found you a delectable dinner," he finished for her, pulling her close. "I've had a hell of a time resisting the appetizers, so I'll start on the first course."

With that, his lips covered hers in a thorough, possessive kiss that made Paige forget all about the congestion at Hyde Park Corner and the heavy noontime traffic at the roundabout.

When John finally raised his head, she found herself breathing hard and clutching his lapels.

"I really think that counted for more than one course," she managed finally.

John had more success controlling his breathing, but his voice was rough as he sat straight again and gave her a rueful look. "Let's hope that it doesn't take as long before we can sample dessert. Many more days like the last ones, and I'll go 'round the bend."

She reached up to feel his forehead in mock concern, and shook her head. "No fever. Are you sure that you're all right?"

"There are some parts of my anatomy that aren't doing too well," he confessed. "Would you kindly go over in your corner of the seat so we can get out at the station without shocking the natives."

She could feel the sudden heat on her cheeks as she met his amused glance, and prudently followed his instruction. "You know what Mrs. Hamilton said—anything goes if it doesn't frighten the horses. All right, all right, I'll behave," she pretended to cower in fright as he raised his hand, "but it's nice to know that I wasn't the only one having to take cold showers." She broke off as he started to laugh. "Now what?"

"I was thinking that taking cold showers wasn't hard at that club. Anything hotter than lukewarm was a bloody miracle, and I should know."

"Umm." She risked a comforting pat on his cheek. "I'd still like to know why your mood has changed faster than English weather. At least on the freighter, you were consistent. You ignored me all the time."

"Which wasn't easy." He peered through the taxi window as the driver slowed and turned into the big gray station. "Let's wait until we get on the train for explanations. It's a shame that we have to board right away." When she stared at him, puzzled, he gave her a wicked grin. "Otherwise we could stand on the platform and indulge ourselves for a short time—nobody thinks a thing about kissing there," John told her solemnly. The taxi slowed to a stop, and he reached for the door. "I'll carry our bags. Can you manage the professor's?"

"Of course." The way she was feeling then, Paige would have tried to straighten the leaning tower of Pisa all by herself. It was only when he added, "For God's sake, don't lose it," that she stared at him over her shoulder. For all his change of mood, it suddenly became obvious that the enigma wasn't over yet.

They were well out of London on the express

train back to Ipswich and the coast, before Paige reached across the seats to firmly take a newspaper from John's hands and say, "I think it's time that we had a little talk. Ever since I've known you, I've felt as if I'd walked into a play after missing the first act. If you don't let me into the scenario soon, I'll trip you when you get off this train and break another rib."

John's firm lips relaxed in a reluctant grin. "I was wondering how much longer you'd hold out." He paused and then leaned down to touch the professor's case at his feet. "This could be the answer to my problem," he said, all traces of humor gone from his face as he stared across at her. "On the other hand, it could be a complete fizzle, and I've struck out again."

"You'll have to go back—I'm still in the middle of the script," she told him. "Maybe I'm dense, but I don't see what my professor's left luggage has to do with anything. You don't even know the man."

"That's right—but Hans does. I've checked the passenger logs, and your professor has sailed on the *Luella Eccles* three times just in the last two years. And you said yourself that he'd told you to get in touch with Hans when you came aboard."

Paige stared at him, bewildered. Finally she said, "Just so I'd have somebody to talk to." Seeing his embarrassed look, she added with satisfaction, "It's going to take you some time to make any brownie points on the trip back. But I don't understand what the chief engineer of a freighter and my boss have in common. Except maybe their age."

"And at the moment, I'd guess their bank

accounts. At least Hans's life-style isn't being provided solely by his Eccles Line paycheck. The company was tipped off sometime ago when inquiries were made about his very hefty bank deposits. All in the last two years."

"Maybe he came into an inheritance," Paige said. "I don't want to rain on your parade, but I still don't see the connection."

"I didn't either, until you mentioned the Bloomsbury bit. Then I thought that was what you and Hans might have been talking about on the way across."

"You should have been listening in," she responded with some asperity. "Practically every sentence included propellers, bent shafts, or how junior engineering officers these days don't know enough to come in out of the rain."

"That's all? He seemed mighty interested in you."

"Word of honor." She put up her hand in mock salute. Then she gave him a thoughtful look. "Wait a minute—if you've been suspicious of Hans, you must have been wondering about me, too. Was that why I was getting the cold and stony?"

John rubbed a finger around his collar, as if it were suddenly uncomfortably tight. "It did occur to me."

She sat forward in her seat, unaware of the English countryside whizzing by outside the train window. "And exactly when did I leave the police lineup in your mind to join the good guys?"

"You're not making this easy for me," John protested.

"I should hope not. All this time, I was wondering what I was doing wrong, and it turns out that I was one of the heavies in the piece."

"Lighten up, will you? I've had a hell of a time."

He sounded so sincere that most of Paige's annoyance evaporated. "Okay," she told him. "I may forgive you eventually. Providing that you tell me how I got off the list of suspects."

"Actually, the clincher was when you would have walked away and left his attaché case in London," he said, nudging it on the floor with his shoe. "Plus the fact that Charleston Farmhouse just brought a 'ho-hum' response from you. No guilty looks or furtive peeks at the empty place on the wall."

"Now I'm more confused than ever," she complained. "What empty place on the wall?"

"The place where the small oil painting by Duncan Grant was hanging before it was stolen earlier this week." He gave her an amused glance. "Did you know that you look a lot like a goldfish with your mouth open?"

Her lips came quickly together in an ominous line. "Now you're beginning to sound like that 'so and so' who occupied the cabin next to mine on the ship." When he started to chuckle, she decided that affronted feminine dignity wasn't going to get her anywhere. "Just tell me what a stolen Duncan Grant painting has to do with all this. And how do you know it's still missing? The guide in the house didn't mention it."

"No, but the lady running the gift shop wasn't so closemouthed. She's enjoying all the excitement from earlier in the week when they discovered the theft."

"I still don't see what this has to do with Hans. He was aboard the ship when all this happened. Unless he has a twin brother, he has a cast-iron alibi—no matter how much money he's deposited in his bank account lately. Besides, that isn't his attaché case, it belongs to the professor—" her voice trailed off as she saw John nod slowly. "Oh, Lord," she whispered, appalled. "You think they're in some skulduggery together?"

"God only knows, but a lot of the things are suddenly fitting together." John sounded tired suddenly. "Last night I found out that Hans had been up to London again, the same time that your room was rifled. He might even have had something to do with that car trying to run me down outside the restaurant earlier."

"But why?" The sound of the train wheels on the track echoed those two words over and over in Paige's mind. Why, why, why?

"Money is the paramount reason, I should think. Or maybe he was afraid we were onto their scheme. I don't know how close Hans came to baring his soul to you on the trip across, but he's convinced fate has dealt him some bitter blows over the years. His wife ran off with another man to start the cycle, and now he feels that he deserves a desk job in the company rather than still going to sea."

"I didn't know all that." Paige was going to ask how he'd gotten so many background facts, and then her thoughts took a different tangent. "Hold on a minute—if Hans and the professor are partners in this thing, why was the attaché case still around? Surely the professor would tell him that he'd left it at the club."

"Of course, but I'm betting that he just said he'd left it for you. It probably didn't occur to either of them that it was still in the storage room, or wherever the porter stashed it."

"But if they didn't find anything in my room, Hans will have to hope that I show up with the case on the ship," she said slowly. "Wouldn't it be easier for us to look inside now?"

John gestured toward it. "That's a sturdy combination lock, and we can't prove a thing by breaking into it when Hans isn't around. Not if we want to nab him."

"On the other hand, we'll feel really stupid if it turns out to contain some dull notes on the Bloomsbury Group and nothing else."

John nodded soberly. "Especially since I've brought in the home office of the company, and they've contacted British authorities, who plan to be aboard in Felixstowe until the ship sails." As the train slowed, he glanced out the window. "Looks as if we're coming in to Ipswich. Time to switch to the local."

"It's too bad we don't have more time here." When he paused in reaching for his raincoat to look at her inquiringly, she went on, "We could use a half hour or so to go and light some candles."

"Try keeping your fingers crossed," John said, getting to his feet as they pulled into the station. "And if you have any voodoo dolls, we could use those, too. Do you want to carry the case while I get our other bags?"

"No way." Paige stood up and reached for her

overnight bag. "I'll be a nervous wreck as it is—for heaven's sake, hang on to it!"

"Don't worry, we'll get it aboard. If my thinking is right, Hans will want to follow their routine and smuggle the picture ashore at the first U.S. port. That must be what he planned all along."

"I certainly hope you're right, although if it comes to a face-off, I think I'd rather be in a crowded railway station than beside the ship's rail in the middle of the English Channel."

"I plan to make damned sure that scenario doesn't happen," John told her, as the train braked to a stop in the Ipswich station and they headed for the open door of the coach.

Chapter Ten

PAIGE WAS SO keyed up by then that every man on
the station concourse in Ipswich looked suspicious.
When the tiny Toonerville Trolley, which serviced
Felixstowe, came in shortly after the express train
departed, she stayed so close to John that she
almost trod on his heels as they went into the middle coach. It was empty until, just before pulling
out of the station, a heavyset man lumbered in to
settle a few dusty seats away. Paige's apprehen-
sive glance sought John's, and they both smiled
with relief when the train conductor greeted the
new arrival as an old acquaintance.

Their short journey passed with hardly any conversation and, although Paige kept her gaze on
the passing scene, she was really unaware of the
tranquil green countryside around them.

When they reached the end of the line at the
English shore resort, they got off and headed
across the track for the taxi stand where three
cars waited. The lead cab was driven by a gray-
haired man who looked as if growing roses would
be more his choice than picking up commuters at
the railway station. When John instructed him to
drive to the container terminal, he merely nodded

in absentminded fashion and watched them struggle their luggage into the small car.

"I'm beginning to feel ridiculous," Paige whispered, once they were settled and the driver pulled away into the town's High Street. "Just as if I'd gotten ready for a horror film, and found that I'd wandered into the kids' matinee instead. The worst part is, I don't know whether to be happy or sad."

John rubbed his forehead wearily. "Let's take it as it comes." He was frowning as the driver turned right to meld with the one-way traffic a block away from the pedestrian mall. "Everything looks pretty deserted for late afternoon."

Paige surveyed the scene, and then let her gaze linger on their driver, who was calmly waving to acquaintances as he drove past. "Probably because it's nearing the dinner hour. Or maybe late teatime. Everything goes to a different schedule over here. That reminds me—what if Hans is still away from the ship?"

"Not a chance. With sailing time so close, a chief engineer is definitely on duty. That is, if he still wants to keep his job with the Eccles Line."

Paige's eyes widened. "You sound awfully sure. Sometime you'll have to tell me your connection with the company." She saw his lips twitch, and she frowned slightly. "Now what's so funny?"

He reached over to take her hand and pull it onto his thigh, where he kept it in a warm, comforting grasp. "Not a thing. A little light relief is great when I've stuck my neck out so far that it's hard to hold my head up."

She moved her fingers to give his a reassuring squeeze. "Don't worry—my money's on you."

"Just your money?" Before she could answer, he glanced around the interior of the cab ruefully. "Never mind—we'll pursue that topic later when there's more room and privacy. Anyhow, it's not much farther now," he added, when they went over the crest of the hill and started down the winding road toward the water. "I can see the container dock from here."

Evidently sight of the ships inspired the driver, because he accelerated so suddenly that Paige was thrown into the corner of the rear seat as he went down the curving road. "What's gotten into him?" she asked John in an undertone as she struggled upright again.

"Who knows? Maybe he believes there's no tomorrow."

"Well, he's doing his best to prove that theory," Paige muttered back. "Thank heavens, we're almost there."

Their Gran Prix run was terminated shortly afterward when the cabbie had to stop at the guarded port gate, while John explained they were passengers on the *Luella Eccles*, which was due to sail shortly.

After the security guard checked his list, he nodded and waved them through the gate. "It's that freighter down at the end of the pier," John instructed their driver. "The one with the diamonds on the stack. Better watch out for the forklifts," he cautioned before the man could accelerate, "the port authorities maintain a strict speed limit in here."

As they pulled alongside the freighter, containers were still being hoisted into the bow of the ship, while a hold cover was being lowered nearer the superstructure. A steady stream of flatbed trucks were pulling away from the forward crane after being divested of their loads to return to the dwindling stack of containers still to be put aboard.

"What do we do now?" Paige asked nervously, once they'd gotten out of the car and the driver had roared off.

John frowned as he surveyed their modest pile of luggage he'd stacked by the end of the gangway. "I suppose the best thing is to leave it here. The guard will call a crewman and have it delivered to our staterooms."

"That's what happened when I boarded in the States," she acknowledged. "But does that mean the briefcase, too?"

"I'm afraid so. Otherwise, it looks as if you're onto the game." John urged her ahead of him up the metal gangway. "Don't worry, we'll keep it under surveillance. Watch it!" he cautioned, and put a firm hand at her back when she slipped on one of the steps.

"Thanks. I'd hate to try this climb in more than two-inch heels. Whoever designs gangways is a real sadist." She knew she was chattering, but it was hard to keep from looking over her shoulder to see if the briefcase was still on the dock.

She managed a smile for the uniformed guard at the top of the gangway, and stood quietly by as John asked him to have their bags delivered up to their cabins.

After going through the heavy metal door leading to the companionway and the decks above, she paused to make sure they were alone and then asked nervously, "Okay, now what do I do?"

"Nothing. Absolutely nothing." He put a hand in the middle of her back to urge her toward the stairway leading up to the lounge and officers' dining area.

"Nothing!" Her response was indignant. Then, she gestured apologetically. "I'm supposed to be in the middle of this."

"Stop arguing." John administered a warning slap on her derriere, so that she had no option but to start up the stairs. "I don't care what you want—your part with that briefcase ceased at the dock. Now go up to your stateroom and lock the door. You're not to open it until I give you the 'all clear.' Got that?"

It was hard to argue when he was urging her up the stairs ahead of him in double time. When they reached the corridor containing the officers' cabins, he paused at the captain's door but gestured her on toward the passenger-deck stairway.

Paige watched him disappear in the captain's stateroom, and then decided it wouldn't hurt to follow orders for a change. Certainly they weren't very difficult ones, she thought as she trudged along the corridor to the steep stairway up to the passenger deck.

There was almost an eerie feeling as she reached the bottom of it. Aside from an occasional jolt when a heavy container was hoisted aboard and the muted rumble of the freighter's engines, it felt as if the ship had been deserted. Probably the off-duty officers were down in the lounge, she reasoned. Either that or sleeping in their cabins before having to take their turns at watch on the return journey.

When she finally reached the top of the stairs, she fumbled in her purse for her stateroom key and then noticed that the door of her cabin was ajar. Cautiously pushing it open, she saw the tall figure of the chief engineer standing by one of the twin beds.

"Ah, Paige," he said calmly. "I thought it was about time you were getting back aboard. I was just checking out your air-conditioning duct before we sailed. We can't have you going from one extreme of temperature to the other the way it was before."

"That's nice of you." Paige tried to keep her voice unconcerned as she tossed her raincoat on the nearest bed. "Have you been on board very long?"

A frown pulled his thick eyebrows together. "Naturally. I'm on duty. Why do you ask?"

"Nothing." She gestured around nervously. "It just seemed so quiet when we came up the gangway."

His look was intent then. "We?"

"Why yes. I caught the same train as John from London, so we shared a taxi from Felixstowe," she said, knowing she wasn't smart enough to think up a good lie on the spur of the moment.

"And where's John now?"

She was proud of her shrug. "Around somewhere. Maybe the captain plans to put him to work this trip. What's funny about that?" she wanted to know as Hans gave a bark of laughter.

"Your friend John evidently didn't bother to mention his middle initial," he said, enjoying her discomfort. "It's *E* for Eccles. Since he heads the company, he's the one who tells people what to do. Or haven't you noticed the VIP treatment he's been getting?"

That bit of information was enough to send Paige's thoughts whirling even faster, and it was an effort not to collapse on the edge of the bed while she assimilated it. Instead, she told herself that it was definitely a case of "first things first." That meant making sure that her luggage and Hans got together without arousing his suspicions.

"I gather he didn't tell you," Hans was going on in a superior tone. "The man's a genius at avoiding involvements. He's spent years perfecting his technique, I hear. Maybe you can confirm that after your London jaunt." He gave her a considering look.

Paige shrugged and managed a rueful response. "Actually, he wasn't around enough to give me any practice." She wandered over to the window of her cabin and glanced toward the dock. "I thought it would be up here by now."

"What are you talking about?"

"My luggage," she responded in a suitably impatient tone. "I'll have to press everything if I can't unpack that bag pretty soon. Maybe I'd better go down and check on it."

He got to the door before her. "I'll run it down for you. Where did you leave it?"

"On the dock." She made a production of peering toward the end of the gangway. "They said somebody would bring it right up."

"There is no need to worry. I'll make sure that it all gets aboard."

"Great!" She flashed a relieved smile his way. "In that case, I'll have a cup of coffee in the lounge—after I comb my hair and put on some lipstick."

She watched him disappear out into the passenger-deck corridor, closing the door behind him. Then she counted to twenty very slowly and followed. With any luck, she could find John and tell him what had transpired before Hans reappeared with the luggage.

She got safely down the stairs to the next deck, thinking that she could use a visit to the lounge as an excuse if she encountered Hans too soon. She hurried along the deserted corridor, but as she came abreast of the captain's cabin, the door opened abruptly and an arm drew her roughly inside. At the same time, a hand clamped over her mouth to muffle her shriek of surprise.

"God damn it, I told you to stay out of things," John muttered angrily in her ear.

Paige sagged in his arms, too relieved to respond in the same vein. A second later though, when his muzzle had been removed, she whispered just as angrily, "Then why didn't you tell me that I'd be entertaining Hans in my cabin?" His astounded expression made her soften her tone. "He's on the way down now to get the luggage."

"The hell he is. It's already been delivered to his cabin." John turned and relayed the information to two individuals who were waiting behind them in the captain's dayroom. One was an attractive middle-aged woman in a stewardess uniform, and the other a brawny young man dressed in casual dock-worker's clothes.

The stewardess went over to the hallway door, which was just barely ajar and held up her hand for silence at the sound of another stateroom door closing and then footsteps along the corridor. "He's taking the other bags up to your deck," she murmured to Paige.

"And the briefcase?"

The woman shook her head. "Which means we'll have to wait just a bit longer I should think. He must intend to open it in his cabin and deliver it later."

"After he's gone through the contents," Paige whispered. She held up crossed fingers. "I hope this works."

"Your part's finished—no matter what happens," John told her firmly. "If you want to do something practical, sit on that couch and—"

His voice trailed off at the sound of returning footsteps on the linoleum-covered corridor. Paige only had time to whisper, "And what?"

"Pray, love," the woman at the door said, barely moving her lips. "Just pray."

Long afterward, Paige remembered her words, but in the five minutes immediately following, all she could recall was the efficiency of the authorities aboard. The "stewardess" allowed Hans only two or three minutes in his cabin before walking in with a passkey to find the chief engineer taking the wraps from a small oil painting. The briefcase that Paige and John had so zealously guarded was open on the bunk behind him.

After that, Hans and the evidence were removed from the ship without delay. A few minutes later, Paige was informed by John that they, too, would be needed in London to testify before the authorities. By then, she found that all her belongings had been removed from the ship and were stacked on the dock ready for a trip back to the city.

This time, she was bundled into the back of a limousine beside John, instead of heading for the train station. All she could think to say as the car pulled away was "I never did get to see that picture."

"Relax, love, I'll let you look at my folio from Charleston again. There's an excellent reproduction at the very front." John stretched his long legs out in front of him, as he relaxed and put a possessive arm around her shoulders. "From here on, I fully intend to complete your education on Duncan Grant's artistic endeavors and a few other topics at the same time. It's apt to take quite awhile."

Paige's breathing seemed to be going faster than the car, as their driver turned onto the highway after leaving the Felixstowe docks. She did manage to swallow and ask, "Exactly how long did you have in mind?" as she felt her head being pulled onto John's shoulder.

"About forty or fifty years should do it," he muttered, using his other hand to position her chin so that her lips would fit nicely under his. "Unless you're a slow learner."

It was a full minute or two later before John

managed to pull back just long enough to mutter, "I'm not sure who'll be teaching who—but who the hell cares?"

The same topic came up again ten days later under considerably different circumstances. By then, they were both occupying the same hotel room in London, but it was on Park Lane rather than Sloane Street. Since John had discovered the fastest way for them to get married in England, they were comfortably planning to celebrate their one-week anniversary later that evening with dinner first and then a visit to the casino. Paige emerged from their bathroom wrapped in a big bath towel to fix an accusing eye on her husband, who was lying atop the king-size bed fiddling with the television remote.

"I look like a prune," she told him accusingly, holding out her hand to illustrate.

He bestowed an amused look while he appraised the stability of her terry-cloth covering. "Then you're the prettiest prune on the block. Besides, when two people share a shower, it's bound to take at least twice as long." He watched a blush go over her cheeks as they both recalled exactly why it took twice as long before he added, "Come over here and let me count the wrinkles."

She raised one eyebrow as she considered his now-familiar form relaxing on the bed. At that moment, it was covered only by a much smaller bath towel. She regretfully shook her head. "I'd better not. We'll miss dinner again if I do."

He didn't stir other than to prop himself more comfortably up on the pillows. "So?"

"We must have set a record for room service as it is," she told him as severely as she could manage.

"All in the line of duty." When she started to laugh, he adopted a solemn tone. "I meant—having to stay here and testify. Once the authorities intercepted your boss at Heathrow, naturally I felt it was my husbandly duty to make sure your name was cleared."

"Naturally," she murmured, sitting down on the end of the bed still out of reach. "Even though he confessed that he and Hans were the only two people involved."

"Hans wasn't happy about that." John's expression sobered as he put the TV remote on the bedside table. "I wonder what will happen next? They've hired some expensive lawyers—that might make a difference in this country, too."

"I wouldn't be too sure of that. They'd been smuggling art out of the country for quite a while, and the British haven't any sense of humor when it comes to losing their national treasures."

John shrugged, and Paige found herself leaning over to touch the smooth tanned skin on his chest. No, more than touching—caressing was a better word. The blush came back as she found herself wanting to keep right on doing it. "I hope your rib is healing properly," she said, avoiding his glance.

"The hell with my rib—come here," he said in a low tone, pulling her down beside him. "Do you realize we only have two days left before we fly home and meet the families?"

"I know." She reached up to gently trace his jaw, and wondered how she ever could have thought it was too stern. "Thank heaven, they all forgave us for getting married in such a rush." Her lips curved in a smile. "I'm glad we didn't have to sail on the freighter as scheduled."

"Since it's doubtful if we would have managed to stay in two separate staterooms until we reached Norfolk, I'd say it was a very good thing, indeed. My reputation would never have survived it," he added solemnly. "Ah—ah—ah," he caught her threatening fist, and managed to pull her closer at the same time. "Besides," he murmured, while carefully divesting her of her covering, "I didn't fancy a seasick bride, and those twin beds leave a lot to be desired."

Paige felt his fingers move possessively down to her hips, and gave a sigh of satisfaction. She relaxed against him while her hand did some wandering of its own. "You do seem to have this thing about beds, Mr. Winthrop, darling."

"Only when the loveliest woman in creation is next to me." He drew in his breath sharply at her touch. "Cut it out, you witch! No, I take it back—don't stop," he replaced her hand, and dropped a quick kiss on her smiling mouth. "Some slow learner you turned out to be! Now, about dinner," he looked at her inquiringly.

"Who needs food? Besides, I like room service," Paige managed breathlessly as she tugged his head down within reach, and felt his hands start to move over her again.

"Possibly a little more practice," he agreed in an uneven voice. "There's never too much of a good thing. Did I mention that I adore you, Mrs. Winthrop?"

"And I adore you," she whispered, as she brushed the edge of his mouth with a loving finger.

"Ummm. Now, hold still and let me kiss you properly."

"That's not proper at all," she managed to get out a few minutes later.

"You're right, my love," he agreed, his voice rough with desire. His lips moved down over her soft, fragrant skin again as if he could never get enough of it, and felt her shiver with delight in response. "Just wonderful—marvelous—and positively—"

"Right, my darling," she assured him. "Oh, so right!"

Tides of Passion

- [ ] **RETURN TO YESTERDAY** by June Lund Shiplett. (121228—$4.99)
- [ ] **JOURNEY TO YESTERDAY** by June Lund Shiplett. (159853—$4.50)
- [ ] **WINDS OF BETRAYAL** by June Lund Shiplett. (150376—$4.99)
- [ ] **THE RAGING WINDS OF HEAVEN** by June Lund Shiplett. (154959—$4.50)
- [ ] **REAP THE BITTER WINDS** by June Lund Shiplett. (150414—$4.50)
- [ ] **THE WILD STORMS OF HEAVEN** by June Lund Shiplett. (126440—$4.99)
- [ ] **SWEET SURRENDER** by Catherine Coulter. (156943—$4.99)
- [ ] **FIRE SONG** by Catherine Coulter. (402383—$4.99)
- [ ] **DEVIL'S EMBRACE** by Catherine Coulter. (141989—$4.99)

Prices slightly higher in Canada

Buy them at your local bookstore or use this convenient coupon for ordering.

NEW AMERICAN LIBRARY
P.O. Box 999, Bergenfield, New Jersey 07621

Please send me the books I have checked above.
I am enclosing $_____ (please add $2.00 to cover postage and handling).
Send check or money order (no cash or C.O.D.'s) or charge by Mastercard or
VISA (with a $15.00 minimum). Prices and numbers are subject to change without
notice.

Card #_____ Exp. Date _____
Signature_____
Name_____
Address_____
City _____ State _____ Zip Code _____

For faster service when ordering by credit card call **1-800-253-6476**

Allow a minimum of 4-6 weeks for delivery. This offer is subject to change without notice.